"You could have called."

He laughed out loud. "When? Before I hit town? You can't possibly be referring to six years ago. I called you plenty after you walked out on me. Remember? You didn't answer. Not once."

She stiffened. "Why are you really here, Nate? And I want the truth."

"Relax, will you? I'm just helping out a family friend. Nothing more."

"Fine."

She appeared unconvinced. Then again, he didn't believe himself, either.

Concern for Samantha might have been the reason he'd initially agreed to his mother's request. But now that he'd arrived in Mustang Valley, he was suddenly determined to find out what he'd done to Ronnie that was so terribly wrong.

She wasn't the entire reason his life had gone from bad to worse to rock bottom, but losing her had surely launched his downward spiral.

Dear Reader,

Some years ago, I lived not far from a Western saloon and restaurant with a small rodeo arena built behind it. The saloon's bull-riding events were a popular weekend attraction, and people would come from hundreds of miles away to both watch and participate. Now, bull riding isn't a sport I would ever attempt, even on an amateur level. I do, however, enjoy watching it—and always cringe when the cowboys are thrown.

I had it in the back of my mind for a long, long time to write a book that included a version of this saloon and restaurant with it's locally famous bull-riding events. The chance finally came with *The Bull Rider's Valentine*—my first-ever book with a Valentine's Day element. Nate Truett, a down-on-his-luck cowboy, lands a job as bull-riding manager. His former girlfriend (and love of his life) happens to be in charge of the barrel-racing events. She's also the one who walked out on him six years ago after his botched Valentine's Day proposal.

Ronnie is the last single Hartman sister to find her happily-ever-after. For me, taking her and Nate from hearts broken to hearts healed was a rewarding journey. Thank you for sharing the ride with us.

Warmest wishes,

Cathy McDavid

Facebook.com/CathyMcDavidBooks

@CathyMcDavid

CathyMcDavid.com

THE BULL RIDER'S VALENTINE

CATHY MCDAVID

HARLEQUIN® WESTERN ROMANCE

Recycling programs
for this product may
not exist in your area.

ISBN-13: 978-1-335-69950-3

The Bull Rider's Valentine

Printed in U.S.A.

www.Harlequin.com

Since 2006, *New York Times* bestselling author **Cathy McDavid** has been happily penning contemporary Westerns for Harlequin. Every day, she gets to write about handsome cowboys riding the range or busting a bronc. It's a tough job, but she's willing to make the sacrifice. Cathy shares her Arizona home with her own real-life sweetheart and a trio of odd pets. Her grown twins have left to embark on lives of their own, and she couldn't be prouder of their accomplishments.

Books by Cathy McDavid

Harlequin Western Romance

Mustang Valley

Harlequin American Romance

Reckless, Arizona

Visit the Author Profile page at Harlequin.com for more titles.

To Pamela, Libby, Connie and Marina.
You not only challenge me to better my writing with
your thoughtful and insightful critiques,
you are my dearest friends.
Your love and support are gifts I truly cherish.

Chapter One

Nate Truett leaned a shoulder against the knotty pine column, drew in a long breath and braced himself for the sight of Ronnie Hartman. He didn't wait long before she emerged from behind a tall paint gelding.

At that moment, two full days of mental preparation promptly deserted him. Nate's heart began to hammer inside his chest. Sweat broke out across his skin, defying the chilly temperature and the heavy canvas jacket he wore. A roaring in his ears drowned out all sound.

He dragged the back of his hand across his damp forehead, wondering what the heck was wrong with him. Ask any of his friends, and they'd say Nate possessed nerves of steel. No one made their living riding eighteen hundred pounds of angry bull into rodeo arenas without them.

Yet where were those nerves of steel now? Weakened, apparently, by the mere sight of an old girlfriend.

The realization that Ronnie still affected him to such a degree was annoying, to say the least. He'd been trying for six years to put his feelings for her where they belonged—in the past.

He'd obviously failed, and miserably at that, as his hammering heart and cold sweat proved.

Pushing back his cowboy hat, he watched Ronnie's every move. She hadn't changed one bit since they'd last seen each other. Still girl-next-door pretty, still wearing her long blond hair in a thick ponytail down her back and still wearing faded red Cardinals hoodies. Next to professional rodeoing, football was her favorite sport.

He swallowed and then groaned softly. Maybe coming to Mustang Valley and agreeing to help his mom's best friend had been a mistake. He considered reversing direction and slinking unnoticed back to where he'd parked his truck in front of the horse stables, but dismissed the idea. He'd made a promise to his mom's friend to check on her daughter, and he would keep that promise no matter how difficult it might be for him.

In another minute. Or two. When he was ready.

Ronnie and her half sister, Samantha, stood beside the paint gelding, which was tethered to an old hitching post. From their gesturing and raised voices, he gathered they were discussing the horse's condition. No surprise. Big John, as Samantha called him, was part of the reason Nate had been asked to make a detour on his trip across Arizona. His mom's friend was worried sick about her oldest, all alone for the first time in her eighteen years.

Learning that Samantha was related to Ronnie had come as a shock to Nate. He'd known Samantha since she was a kid and also that she was adopted. There was never a mention of her seeking out her biological family, which she'd done after graduating high school. It must have come as a bigger shock to Ronnie, who until recently had no idea Samantha existed. Or that her father had a child with his then girlfriend and didn't tell anyone.

Nate wondered how Ronnie was coping in the wake of the bombshell news but doubted she'd tell him. He'd be lucky if she discussed even the weather with him. Ronnie was an expert at erecting emotional barricades and didn't easily take them down. Nate had learned that firsthand the hard way.

All at once, Samantha unleashed her teenage fury on Ronnie, shouting, "You don't care about me! You've never cared! You just want me to win using your horse so you can sell him for a lot of money!" She ended her outburst with a sob. When Ronnie attempted to put an arm around Samantha, she jerked away. "Leave me alone."

Nate straightened but didn't otherwise move. Samantha could be a bit of a drama queen—even before learning the man who'd raised her wasn't her real father. But when the loud wails continued, he hurried down the ranch office steps and toward the pair. No way was he letting anxiety over his past relationship with Ronnie, or the fact she was Samantha's half sister, interfere with the purpose of his visit—namely, seeing how Samantha was doing and lending assistance if needed.

He'd almost reached the pair when Ronnie abruptly pivoted and caught sight of him. Surprise sparked in her vivid green eyes, followed by alarm. Both emotions dimmed as she visibly gained control.

"Nate! What are you doing here?"

Really? No "Hello" or "Hi" or "How are you?" He couldn't let that slide. Flashing the same wide grin that had at one time been plastered on billboards and the cover of *Pro Rodeo Sports News*, he said, "Nice to see you, too, Ronnie."

Whatever she intended to say was cut short by Samantha, who whirled and exclaimed, "Nate, you came!" before rushing forward to give him a hug. "I'm so glad. Mom said you might, but she wasn't sure."

Nate grabbed the teenager before she knocked him over. "Hey there, Sammy-cakes." Giving her a brotherly squeeze, he set her aside.

Ronnie stared at him, her expression unyielding and her arms crossed. Not that he'd expected a warm welcome, considering she'd walked out on him without so much as a "See ya later."

Still, they'd been close once. Close enough to live together, suffer through an unbearable loss and for Nate to propose.

He'd planned the entire Valentine's Day dinner, right down to the ring and the moment he'd pop the question over dessert. Her rejection had stunned him. Not as much, however, as coming home two days later to discover her gone, along with all her clothes and possessions.

Happy freakin' Valentine's Day to him.

"Wait, wait." Ronnie drew back, her narrowed gaze traveling from Nate to Samantha. "What is happening here?"

Nate sighed. "You didn't tell her I was coming?"

"Well… I…got busy…" Samantha faltered. "And forgot."

"You two are friends?" Ronnie asked, clearly mystified.

"My mom and Nate's are best friends from when we lived in Abilene." Samantha lifted one shoulder in an unconcerned shrug.

"But you're from Flagstaff." Ronnie spoke slowly.

"We just moved there last year."

"Small world, huh?" Nate hadn't often enjoyed the upper hand with Ronnie and, to be honest, he kind of liked it.

"Very small."

"Well, you were only in Abilene a year. And we were traveling almost every weekend. You never got a chance to meet Mom's friends."

Samantha stared curiously at Ronnie and Nate. "So, I'm guessing you two are more than just rodeo acquaintances. That's what Mom said."

Nate waited for Ronnie to admit they'd dated for three years and lived together for one.

After a long, uncomfortable pause, she said, "Nate and I met when we were both competing on the circuit."

That was it? No details?

"Of course." Samantha's wide smile said she wasn't buying the vague explanation for one second.

"Of course," Nate repeated, remembering the first time he'd seen her.

It had been at the New Mexico State Fair. He'd been competing professionally for almost two years while Ronnie was a newcomer. He'd asked her out three times over the next three rodeos before she finally accepted. After that, they were rarely apart.

Ronnie must have been remembering, too, for she shifted nervously and changed the subject. "What are you doing in Mustang Valley?"

"I stopped on my way to Houston." He, too, was purposefully vague. Let her think what she would. He didn't owe her or anyone an explanation. "Sam's mom said she was upset about her horse. Mom thought I could help and asked me to stop. Lend some support."

"I see." Ronnie faced Samantha. "You really should have told me Nate was coming."

"Like I said, I didn't know for sure."

Nate doubted her but kept his mouth shut. Instead, he asked, "What's going on with Big John?"

"I think he's perfectly fine to compete this weekend. Ronnie says no."

"Has he fully healed?"

"Yes," Samantha blurted at the same time Ronnie said, "No."

Nate knew that four months ago the horse had suffered a torn ligament and been sidelined for what was supposed to be the rest of the year. Naturally, Samantha had been devastated.

"What does Mel say? She's the medical expert." Deferring to Ronnie's older sister, who was also the small town's sole veterinarian, made sense.

"She agrees with me that competing on him right now is risky." Ronnie studied the horse, whose quiet patience and idly swishing tail belied his winning speed and agility in the arena. "He still exhibits tenderness in the affected area."

"He's ready," Samantha insisted. "I ran him three times earlier today. His time was almost as fast as before."

Ronnie went slack-jawed. "You ran him and didn't tell me?"

"You were busy."

"He might have reinjured that leg." She didn't hold back and returned Samantha's earlier fury. "Are you crazy?"

"He's my horse."

"He could be your lame-for-life horse."

Samantha started crying again. "What if I don't qualify for Nationals?"

"There's always next year. You only just turned professional this past spring."

Nate didn't entirely blame Ronnie for being angry. As a trainer, she cared enormously about the welfare of her horses and those under her care. Also, in this case, she happened to be right. He'd seen more than one horse's career ruined by pushing for too much too soon.

"You said you'd help me." Samantha sniffed and wiped her eyes.

"You sure you're not just panicking?" Nate decided the time had come for him to step in and do what he'd been asked. "There are only two weekends left to compete."

"I'm not panicking." Her tone said otherwise. "I have

to place in at least one of those rodeos or I'm done for the year."

"Your mom says you're doing great on Ronnie's horse."

"Not great enough. I need Big John."

What she probably needed was a confidence boost. Nate had dozens of friends who'd suffered a similar crisis at one point or another in their careers. It was a common enough affliction on the circuit. Never happened to him, however. All his crises had come after he'd retired.

"I have a suggestion. Why don't you take Ronnie's horse on a couple of runs? Let me get a firsthand look at the two of you working together."

"That's not a bad idea," Ronnie said.

Did she just agree with him? Well, knock him sideways with a feather.

"Okay. Be right back." Samantha left, half running, half jogging to the stables where Nate presumed Ronnie's horse was kept. Her long blond hair, so much like Ronnie's, lifted in the wind.

How had he not noticed the resemblance between the two of them years before? It seemed so obvious now. Then again, why would he have? If not for Samantha's search for her biological father, they'd all still be in the dark.

"What about Big John?" Ronnie called after Samantha.

"I'll get him later."

Ronnie could have untied the horse and taken him back to his stall, leaving Nate to fend for himself. But she didn't. Wasn't that interesting?

"Alone at last," he teased.

"Not funny."

"Come on, I was just as surprised to learn Samantha's your sister as you were."

"And what? You wanted to see for yourself?"

"You think I showed up here on purpose? Because I can assure you, the idea was entirely Mom's. I had no intention of ever setting foot in Mustang Valley again."

She studied him intently, revealing the barest hint of vulnerability before averting her glance. Why, for crying out loud? She was the one who'd dumped him. And without good reason, he might add. Without *any* reason.

"You could have called."

He laughed out loud. "When? Before I hit town? You can't possibly be referring to six years ago. I called you plenty after you walked out on me. Remember? You didn't answer. Not once."

She stiffened. "Why are you really here, Nate? And I want the truth."

"Relax, will you? I'm just helping out a family friend. Nothing more. Samantha's like a little cousin to me."

"Fine."

She appeared unconvinced. Then again, he didn't believe himself, either.

Concern for Samantha might have been the reason he'd initially agreed to his mother's request. But now that he'd arrived in Mustang Valley, he was suddenly determined to find out what he'd done to Ronnie that was so terribly wrong.

She wasn't the entire reason his life had gone from bad to worse to rock bottom, but losing her had surely launched his downward spiral.

THE LAST PERSON Ronnie had expected to see today—*any* day, truth be told—was Nate Truett. Not after she'd left him with no explanation.

He should hate her and probably did. That didn't stop him from being the one guy she'd struggled to forget and couldn't. The one who made every man she met pale in comparison.

Now, here he stood, not eighteen inches away from her and wearing the same heart-stopping, tummy-fluttering smile that had caused her to fall for him in the first place.

"What are you thinking?" he asked in the husky drawl that still invaded her dreams.

"Nothing."

I hurt you badly, and I'm sorry. I shouldn't have just walked out like that. It was wrong and not what you deserved. But nothing's changed.

"Sam," she amended. Safe conversation gave nothing away while ignoring him would reveal too much.

"Sam?"

"You know my dad. Nicknames for all his daughters."

"I'd forgotten, *Rhonda*."

She rolled her eyes, wishing she'd never told him. "Sam has a lot of talent. She can also be stubborn to a fault."

"I wonder where she gets that?" Nate moved marginally closer.

Ronnie stilled, acutely aware of him. "I'm only stubborn when I'm right."

"Which, if memory serves, is always."

"Not true." Sorrow consumed her. "I'm sure you haven't forgotten."

"Ronnie."

She forced herself to stroll casually away, intent on removing herself from his rugged good looks, aw-shucks charm and dancing blue eyes that by all counts should be outlawed. Naturally, he followed her, further weakening her already vulnerable state.

Heaving a soft groan, she reached for the top railing of the arena fence, using it to steady her wobbly knees. If she weren't careful, Nate might realize her feelings for him weren't completely extinguished. His ego was already big enough.

At least, it used to be. He did seem a bit more…humble than before, something she found both out of character and intriguing.

"Big John is a valuable horse," she said, staring off at the distant McDowell Mountains. Anywhere other than at Nate. "I'd hate to see him turned into a kid's mount because of an injury."

"I agree. Championship horses cost a lot of money. I doubt Samantha can afford to buy a new one." He lowered his voice to the range that had always sent a delicious tingle skittering up her spine. "It's really nice of you to let her borrow your horse."

She started to tell him more about Sam's sudden appearance this past summer and how she, Mel and Frankie had been devastated to learn their father had lied to them for nearly two decades. At the last second, she bit her tongue. She and Nate didn't have that kind of relationship anymore.

"How are your sisters?" he asked. "They were always a hoot and a half."

"Fine."

"Just fine?"

"What did Sam's mom tell you?" She spared him a quick glance.

"That besides starting her own vet practice, Mel got married, and Frankie has twin girls."

There was actually considerably more, such as Mel being pregnant, Frankie's new catering business, the recent return of the twins' father and the sizable amount of money Ronnie's father had won in the state lottery. She mentioned none of it.

Nate reached for her left hand, sending a sudden zing racing through her system. She clamped her mouth shut before a gasp escaped.

"What are you doing!" she demanded.

"No wedding ring, I see."

Bristling, she reclaimed her hand. "Sam's mom skip that part?"

"As a matter of fact, she didn't."

"Then why—" She abruptly stopped when he broke into laughter. "You're such a..." Damn him for flustering her.

"Can't blame me for trying. You always had the softest skin."

"How long are you staying in Mustang Valley?"

As intended, her question sobered him. "I'm not sure. A couple days. Possibly longer. It all depends."

"On what?" *Please don't say me.*

"Sam, for starters."

She resisted asking what else. "I thought you were heading to Houston."

"There's no rush."

The humbleness Ronnie had noticed before returned. Though, on second thought, she decided it might be something else. Embarrassment, possibly? Or secrecy? For whatever reason, Nate was definitely holding back.

"Where are you staying?" she asked.

That earned her a lengthy once-over. "Why do you care?"

"I'm not coming over, if that's what you're hinting at."

"Darn it." He feigned disappointment. "Foiled again."

"Seriously, Nate. There's the Morning Side Inn."

For a moment, he appeared as if he might deliver another jab. Instead, his expression changed and he said, "I have my horse trailer. The one with living quarters. I just need to find a place to park it. Hopefully, near wherever I wind up boarding Breeze."

Ronnie's determination to remain indifferent instantly dissolved. "You still have Breeze? How old is she now? I figured you might have retired her."

"She's twenty-one. And retired, other than pleasure riding. I thought about leaving her at my folks' place."

"Except you couldn't bear to part with her." Ronnie was admittedly touched.

"We've been together a long time."

Nate had owned the mare since he'd competed on the junior circuit in high school. Besides rising to bull and bronc riding fame, he'd also won multiple steer wrestling championships—all of them on Breeze.

"The Morning Side Inn has stalls to lease," she offered.

"We'll see." Again, his expression changed, as if he were hiding something.

Ronnie had to ask. "Is Sam the only reason you came?"

He hesitated briefly before saying, "It's enough of a reason."

His lack of a real answer worried her.

"Are you and Sam close?"

She'd yet to wrap her brain around the incredible coincidence that her half sister was the daughter of his mom's best friend. She'd met his parents a few times, naturally, just like he'd met her dad and sisters when they'd visited Mustang Valley. But never his mom's best friend and certainly not Sam.

"Not especially close," he said. "I'd see her at holiday dinners and birthday parties. But her mom is a good friend to mine. She helped us a lot after Allan passed."

Ronnie hadn't known Nate's brother; he'd died from cystic fibrosis before she and Nate met. But Nate had frequently talked about Allan and the mark both he and his absence had left on Nate's life.

"Sam and her parents aren't getting along too well these days," Ronnie said. "Did your mom mention that, too? According to Sam, it's because they don't support her decision to skip college and become a professional barrel racer."

"They also weren't crazy about her running off in search of your dad without mentioning a word to them."

Ronnie hadn't been crazy about Sam finding their father, either. Not in the beginning. Learning he'd been involved with a younger woman *and* had a child with her took a lot of getting used to.

"Trust me," she said. "The news was a shock to all of us."

"She's lucky." For the first time since Ronnie had reclaimed her hand from his, Nate looked at her. "Not all biological families are as accepting as yours."

"None of what happened was her fault. We weren't about to hold the mistakes our respective parents made against her." A thought occurred to Ronnie. "Did your mom know about my dad? Did you?"

"No. We were as surprised as anyone."

At that moment, Sam emerged from the stables astride Ronnie's horse, Comanche. The handsome, muscular gelding might not be Sam's first choice, but no one could deny the pair made an impression as she trotted him toward the arena. One of the ranch hands, who happened to be in the vicinity, opened the gate for her.

Fortunately, no one else was practicing at this time of day. In another six weeks, when school let out for winter break, Powell Ranch would be packed from morning until evening.

"You ready?" Sam hollered from her position at the south end of the arena.

Nate took out his phone and opened the stopwatch app. "All set," he hollered back.

Sam studied the cloverleaf course while adjusting her weight in the saddle.

"Take your time," Ronnie muttered under her breath. "Don't rush."

Comanche stared straight ahead, nervously prancing in place. He knew his job and was eagerly awaiting the signal from Sam. The next second, she gave it. Trotting him in a tight circle, she suddenly spurred him into a full-speed-ahead gallop and made for the first barrel.

Ronnie glanced briefly at Nate to confirm what she already knew—that he was timing Sam's run.

How often had he done the same for her when she'd been practicing? She couldn't begin to count. During the years they'd been together, he'd supported her tirelessly and without fail.

Until the day she'd miscarried and their world had changed.

Her fault. Entirely. He'd tried hard to make things right by proposing two months later on Valentine's Day. In her mind, she saw the small, red velvet box and the glittering heart-shaped diamond ring. So very pretty. She'd needed all her willpower to tell him no.

As one would expect, he'd been crushed and unable to accept that their relationship was too broken to fix. But Ronnie had, and two days later, she'd left him and the place they'd shared in Abilene behind, convinced a quick and clean parting was best for both of them.

Sadly, she'd been mistaken. Those dozens of voice

mail messages he'd left had been filled with pain and
anguish. And for months afterward, mutual friends had
had nothing good to report, saying Nate had stopped
competing, dropped out of sight and broken the terms of
multiple endorsement contracts. By the following year,
their mutual friends had had no idea where he was or
what had happened to him.

Ronnie had tried telling herself the same thing would
have happened regardless of how delicately she'd handled
the breakup. Sometimes, she almost believed it. Mostly,
she regretted her actions. Nate had done nothing wrong,
was, in fact, a great boyfriend and had been deserving
of far more from her. She'd been the one consumed by
grief and guilt. The one who'd wanted out.

"Whoo-hoo!" Sam gave a loud hoot as she rounded
the last barrel and galloped for the finish line.

Head stretched out and tail flying, the Comanche ran
for all he was worth. Crossing the finish line, Sam slowed
the horse as they passed through the gate, then brought
him back around.

Ronnie didn't have to wait for Nate's announcement.
Instinct, honed from years of competing, followed by
years of teaching, told her Sam's time was in the money.

"Sixteen-point-three-six seconds." He showed her the
phone. "Not bad for a pattern this size."

"From what Sam has told me, that's very close to Big
John's time pre-injury."

"Meaning she can do as well on Comanche as Big
John."

Ronnie pushed off the arena fence. "If she wants.
Which she doesn't."

"Put yourself in her shoes. What was it like when
you competed on a horse that wasn't yours? It can be
intimidating."

Before Ronnie could respond, Sam trotted over, Comanche's sides continuing to heave from his exertion. With nimble ease, she jumped off, the reins loosely clutched between her fingers. "How'd we do?"

Nate told her.

She frowned. "Better than I thought."

"Then why are you mad?"

"I'm not."

Except, she was. If Ronnie were to guess, she'd say the horse's more than decent performance hadn't bolstered Sam's argument that she needed Big John in order to qualify for Nationals.

Nate pocketed his phone. "You were a little slow changing leads on that last barrel."

Ronnie had also noticed the lag but refrained from commenting. She and Sam regularly engaged in this same argument. Sam always blamed the horse and did again today.

"It's not my fault. I have to cue him twice before he changes leads."

"Maybe you need to practice more. The partnership between horse and rider doesn't happen overnight. It can take months, years even, to perfect."

Something else Ronnie had tried to tell Sam, without much success.

"You're right." The teenager flashed Nate an apologetic smile. "I can't help getting impatient."

What? Ronnie blinked. Had Sam really just agreed with Nate when all she ever did with Ronnie was fight? Increasingly so these last weeks as the competitive season drew nearer and nearer to an end.

"Will you stay the next two weeks and help me?" She grabbed Nate's arm with her free hand. "Please. I know I can qualify with you coaching me."

Coaching her? Wasn't that Ronnie's job?

She coughed and cleared her throat. "I think Nate's on his way to Houston."

"That can wait." He sent her a look that probably wasn't dismissive but felt that way nonetheless.

"Yes." Sam's face exploded in a huge smile. "I'm so happy."

Not Ronnie. "We wouldn't wish to inconvenience you," she said dryly.

"No inconvenience. I'll juggle my schedule."

If only she could do the same and leave town for the next two weeks. Unfortunately, obligations to her family, her barrel racing business and her students kept her rooted in Mustang Valley for the foreseeable future.

A future that, temporarily at least, now included Nate Truett.

Chapter Two

"Where's the rodeo this weekend?" Nate asked. He led Breeze while Samantha—he supposed he should get used to calling her Sam—walked beside him. They'd been circling the grounds for the last fifteen minutes, letting the old mare stretch her legs a bit before returning her to the trailer.

"Kingman. The Annual Andy Devine Days. We need to be on the road no later than 6:00 a.m. Friday morning."

That gave him the rest of today, plus Wednesday and Thursday, to find a place to park his trailer and earn some quick cash.

"I like Kingman. Those were the days..."

"Was that where you earned your first championship?" she asked.

"Hardly. But I did win my first buckle there. In steer wrestling."

"Not bull riding?"

"If I recall correctly, I came in dead last."

"No way!"

"It's true." He'd been all of eighteen and, just like Sam, brand new to professional rodeoing. "I lasted a whopping one-point-two seconds before T-Rex dumped me face-first into the dirt."

"You remember the bull's name?"

"He made an impression."

The truth was, Nate had been scared witless when T-Rex executed an abrupt one-eighty and charged. It was without doubt the quickest he'd ever scrambled to his feet and scaled the fence. The small scar on his left shin was a constant reminder of just how close the bull's hoof had come to slicing his leg open.

"We'll probably take Ronnie's truck and trailer to Kingman," Sam said. "Is that okay with you? There's enough room for all of us to bunk in the camper."

"I'll get a hotel room." Not that he had much money for a hotel. Unless his luck changed.

"Okay. If you're sure."

"I am." Sure that Ronnie wouldn't bunk in the same camper with him even if her life depended on it.

He and Sam turned the corner of the horse barn, trading late October sunshine for chilly shade. Ronnie hadn't come with them. She'd made some excuse about returning a phone call and hightailed it to the ranch office. From the look on Ronnie's face when he'd accepted Sam's invitation to stay, she needed some alone time to process this unexpected development.

Not nice of him, for sure. He really should have called ahead and given her fair warning. Only, deep down, a small part of him still resented her for rejecting his proposal, and for her brutal handling of their breakup—which must mean an equally small part of him still cared for her. Not that he'd admit as much, to her or anyone else.

At his truck, Sam held Breeze's lead rope while Nate lowered the trailer's rear gate. With very little prodding, the old brown mare meandered in and waited for Nate to secure her lead rope to the metal ring.

"Are there any cheap places in the area I can park my trailer? Preferably one that rents spaces by the day or week."

"Why not stay at Ronnie's?" Sam offered. "She has room. There's just her now that Mel moved out. And since you two already know each other—"

"Room for what?"

Nate and Sam both turned at the sound of Ronnie's voice. "Nothing," he said, hoping Sam took the hint and kept quiet.

She didn't. "Can Nate park his truck and trailer at your house?"

"Um…ah…"

"Don't worry about it." Nate let Ronnie off the hook with a casual wave. "I'll find something. Besides, I need a place for Breeze, too."

"She has an empty stall," Sam persisted.

Ronnie shook her head. "I don't think that's a good idea."

"Why not?"

"Because it's my house, and I get to decide who stays. Not you."

"You're saying no just because I asked," Sam complained, clearly not liking that her idea was being shot down. "And because I want to use Big John instead of your horse."

"Trust me, those aren't the reasons."

"Then what is?"

"Sam, drop it." Nate put just enough bite in his voice to get her attention. "I won't be the cause of a problem between you and your sister. If that's the case, I'll leave."

Sam clamped her jaw shut and rolled her eyes. "She's impossible. I can't do anything right, lately."

"Not the time or place," Ronnie warned.

"Fine. I'll ask Frankie." Sam pulled her cell phone from her pocket and tapped in a number before Ronnie could object. "I'm staying with her, anyway, and *she* has room for another horse."

Nate tried again to stop her. "It's okay. Really. I'll find a place."

She was too busy making the call to listen.

"Sorry about this." He smiled apologetically at Ronnie while Sam waited for the eldest Hartman sister to answer.

"On the off chance Frankie agrees, I'd appreciate it if you decline."

For no reason Nate could come up with, Ronnie's request irked him. "I'm not trying to make trouble for you."

"And, yet, you are."

"Hi, Frankie," Sam chirped. "Sorry to bother you at work." Nate and Ronnie exchanged glances while Sam made her plea. "I promise, it would only be for a couple of days. A week at the most."

"Tell her I'll pay rent." And Nate would, the moment he found work.

Emotion sparked in Ronnie's eyes, but she said nothing. Rather, she stepped up onto the trailer's running board, reached inside and began petting Breeze. The old horse snorted and closed her eyes, thoroughly enjoying the head scratching.

"You're a good girl, aren't you?" Ronnie cooed.

Nate's anger faded. Ronnie had once doted on Breeze almost as much as he did.

"Sure. Of course." Sam's gaze cut to Nate. "I will. Thanks." She disconnected. "Frankie says you and she can talk about it when you get there."

"Great." Not a yes exactly. Then again, not a no. With limited options, he decided he'd agree to whatever terms Frankie named, within reason.

Ronnie huffed in disgust.

"I could ride back with you," Sam suggested. "Save Ronnie from having to drive me."

"Sure."

"Can we take Big John, too? Since I won't be riding him at Kingman this weekend, might as well take him home." The last part included a not-so-subtle jab directed at Ronnie.

"Let's load up, then. It's getting close to dinnertime. I don't want to interfere with Frankie's schedule."

Ronnie hopped down from the running board. "What about practice tomorrow?" Her voice was strained, but civil.

"I'm taking the twins to preschool, and then helping Mel until two. She needs some lab tests dropped off at FedEx."

Nate's mom had mentioned something about Sam working for her sisters in exchange for room and board and Big John's vet care. Again, he reflected on how lucky the teenager was to have such a willing and welcoming biological family, bickering with Ronnie aside.

"There are only a few days left before we leave," Ronnie said. "You can't afford to miss any practice."

"I get it." Sam's tone was sharp. "I'll be here. Two thirty."

"All right." Ronnie started to leave, then paused to look at Nate. "Both of you, I'm assuming."

"Wouldn't miss it." He slung a brotherly arm around Sam's shoulders, hoping to incite a rise from Ronnie.

He got it. She sucked in a harsh breath before pivoting on her heel.

Sam watched her go. "She can be pretty uptight sometimes."

"She always was."

"I'm assuming you were, like, boyfriend and girlfriend."

"Yeah." He hadn't planned on admitting even that much. "How'd you guess?"

"It's kind of obvious."

"Hmm. Apparently, I need to try harder."

"When did you two date?"

"Six years ago."

"What happened?"

"We drifted apart." What else was there to say when he had no clue what had prompted Ronnie to pack up and leave with no warning? She'd obviously fallen out of love and fast.

"She doesn't date," Sam said. "Not since I've been here, anyway."

"She's busy. Running a barrel racing school takes a lot of time."

"Guys ask her. I've overheard 'em. And Mel and Frankie are always telling her she needs to get out more."

Nate believed it. Mustang Valley was nothing if not a cowboy town. In addition to the various horse ranches, there were five sizable cattle ranches in the area and as many more within a thirty-mile radius. A gal as pretty as Ronnie must have her pick of men.

"She's always telling them no." Sam followed him to the front compartment where he secured a latch.

"I really don't care about her social life."

"But don't you think it's strange? I've only been living here since the summer, and I've gone out with two different guys."

He paused and gave her a serious look. "Anybody I have to beat up for getting out of line?"

"Will you quit it?" She groaned.

"Come on, we need to hit the road. Where's Big John?"

"I'll be right back."

Not long after that, Big John had been loaded beside Breeze, who'd readily accepted her new traveling companion. Nate carefully navigated the long, winding road from Powell Ranch down the mountainside. Sam sat beside him, chatting up a storm and pointing out some of the local sights. He'd been to Mustang Valley twice before, back in the days when he and Ronnie were together. A lot had changed, however, and he appreciated the update.

Frankie's house was in one of the new subdivisions on the other side of the valley and, according to Sam, had a mini barn and horse setup. She directed Nate down a side access road where Frankie waited by an open RV gate. She motioned for him to enter and park his trailer in a spot that butted up beside the covered horse stalls.

He took his time, being extra careful not to hit anything. At last satisfied with the trailer's position, he shut off the engine and exited the cab. Sam did the same. Later, after he and Frankie had a chance to talk, he'd unhitch the truck from his trailer and park it on the street.

"Hi, Frankie." He considered giving her a hug when she met up with him in front of his truck. At the last second, he reconsidered and reached out his hand. "I really appreciate this."

She returned his handshake with genuine warmth. "I wish it could be longer, but I can only let you stay until Monday."

Sam had left that part out. Well, no matter. It was enough he had a place for the next four days.

"Did Sam tell you, I insist on paying rent?"

"She did, and I won't hear of it. You can help with chores and maybe some repairs."

"Anything you need."

The teenager scurried about, unloading Big John first and taking him to his stall.

"In the meantime," Frankie said, "you'll find a garden hose and heavy-duty electrical cord in the tack room. It's unlocked. There's an outlet over there." She pointed to the side of the small barn. "And the closest water spigot is by the corral."

Nate tugged on the brim of his cowboy hat. "I can't thank you enough."

"When you've finished, come knock on the door. I've got supper in the oven, and you can meet my daughters. Spence, too, if he gets home in time."

"I don't expect you to feed me." Though Nate wouldn't mind. His lunch had consisted of a stale leftover doughnut.

She ignored his protest. "And while we're eating, you can tell me the real reason you're here."

He surprised himself by agreeing. "And maybe in exchange, you can tell me about Ronnie."

TWO PAIRS OF EYES, one of them brown and the other one green, stared at Nate from across the kitchen table. Weren't twins supposed to look alike? Frankie's two certainly didn't.

"We're four," the smaller one announced and held up the appropriate number of fingers.

"Not yet," Frankie corrected as she set plates in front of them. "In a couple of weeks."

The little girl giggled impishly and then, like her sister, dug into her food. Nate did as well, after Frankie had taken her seat. Waiting wasn't easy.

"This is good." In fact, he couldn't remember when he'd tasted better meat loaf.

"Mommy caters food," the smaller girl said around a swallow of milk.

Did the taller one ever talk?

"Is that so?" Nate asked.

"I-Hart-Catering. H-A-R-T. Like our last name."

"Clever. And congratulations on your new business.

Sam raved about it on the drive over here. Said you're really picking up steam."

He'd expected the teenager to join them for dinner, only to learn she'd made plans with a friend. Spence, Frankie's fiancé, and the father of her daughters, was working late at the horse racing farm where he was head trainer. That left just her, the twins and Nate.

The slight discomfort he'd initially felt at being alone with them—not to mention his anxiety about the questions Frankie might pose—had been vanquished by the hospitality she'd shown. Hospitality that included feeding him an incredible home-cooked meal.

"Thanks." She stopped to reprimand the girls for sneaking their vegetables to the dogs beneath the table. "I only just got I-Hart-Catering off the ground. Time will tell if I can make a go of it."

He savored a mouthful of superbly seasoned green beans. "With food this good, I don't see how you can fail."

"It's not easy. I'm still working full-time at the café and catering mostly on weekends. That may change if things keep going like they are."

"Well, good luck to you."

She gave her head an incredulous shake. "I still can't believe your mom and Sam's mom are such good friends. What are the odds?"

"Beyond my limited math skills."

"I wonder why Ronnie didn't make the connection when Sam first arrived."

"Well, they never met. And while I'm sure I mentioned Sam's mom, I doubt her last name ever came up."

"Did Sam tell you how she found us?"

"She said your dad won the state lottery earlier this year and she tracked him down online."

The story was an interesting one, and Frankie recounted it while they ate.

"He split the winnings four ways. It wasn't a fortune but enough to better all of our lives. I bought this house with my share. Mel acquired her veterinary practice. Dad paid for his wedding to Dolores and for their honeymoon. And Ronnie started her barrel racing school. Before that she worked for the Powells, teaching classes and training horses. Because the money was spent before Sam got here, we all pitch in to help cover her rodeo expenses. She, in turn, helps us out as much as she can in exchange for room and board and Big John's medical costs."

"Must have been a shock, learning you had a half sister."

"*Quite* a shock. But we adapted quickly." Frankie set her fork down. "All right, not that quickly. But that's to be expected."

"Have she and Ronnie always squabbled like they do?"

"Funny you should mention that. No, they haven't. Just lately. Sam's really worried she won't qualify for Nationals, and Ronnie's trying hard to get her there. That's probably putting a strain on their relationship."

Nate thought back on his own rodeo career. In hindsight, he'd never worried much about qualifying. If it happened, great, if not, no big deal. He'd competed strictly for fun. That he'd earned a long list of titles and made decent money by anyone's standards had often amazed him.

He had his late brother, Allan, to thank. Knowing his life would end prematurely, Allan had instilled Nate with a seize-the-moment attitude, and for many years Nate embraced the philosophy. He'd also reaped the rewards.

But Allan hadn't lived long enough to learn the higher one flew, the farther they fell, and the more difficult it was for them to recover.

"Maybe the reason Ronnie and Sam bicker is because they're a lot alike."

Frankie stared at him as if he'd just solved a difficult scientific equation. "You're absolutely right. Can't imagine why that didn't occur to me before. Those two are peas in a pod."

The taller twin spoke for the first time. "What's a pod, Mommy?"

While Frankie explained, the four of them finished their dinner. Afterward, she dispatched the girls to the family room to play.

"Can I help with cleanup?" Nate asked.

"An offer I never turn down."

Their friendly conversation continued, centering on Ronnie and Nate's rodeo days and the good memories, of which there were many. During a break, Nate asked Frankie the question that had been bothering him from the moment his mom called and requested he stop in Mustang Valley.

"Do you have any idea why Ronnie took off without even leaving a goodbye note?"

Frankie stopped loading the dishwasher. "You really should talk to her."

"I tried, believe me. Kind of hard when she wouldn't return my phone calls. I'm hoping to ask her when the moment's right."

"If it makes you feel better, she hardly spoke to any of us after she came back." Frankie's expression turned sad. "She took the miscarriage really hard."

"She wasn't the only one."

"Oh, Nate. I'm so sorry. Shame on us for thinking just of Ronnie and not you."

He'd been surprised by his excitement at the prospect of becoming a father, considering how young he and

Ronnie both were and the pregnancy being completely unplanned. He'd figured on having kids in the distant future, not at twenty-four and when his career was just beginning to peak.

"Ronnie really wanted the baby," Frankie said. "I know that for a fact."

"Then why did she insist on competing?" It made no sense to him, then or now.

"I can only guess. I know the decision wasn't easy for her and when things went...wrong, she was devastated."

Nate had been watching from the arena fence as Ronnie executed her run, his muscles clenching at every tight turn she made around the barrels. He'd gone weak as a pup when, after completing the run, she reined her horse to a stop and climbed off safely.

Then, the unthinkable happened. While she stood watching the remaining competitors and chatting with friends, a runaway horse appeared from out of nowhere and nearly ran her over, causing her to trip and fall.

They'd seen the on-site medic and thought she was fine. But a few hours later, he'd rushed Ronnie to the hospital where she lost the baby.

"I did everything I could to support her," Nate said, using a trip to the table for dirty dishes to gain control of his emotions.

"I have no doubt." Frankie finished loading the dishwasher. Closing the door, she leaned her hip against the counter. "She did say your mother was...harsh when expressing her opinion."

His parents had arrived at the hospital the next morning just before Ronnie was to be released. His mother had been thrilled about the baby and couldn't wait for the arrival of her first grandchild. But rather than comfort Ronnie, she'd made callous remarks about Ronnie not being ready for motherhood and selfishly putting her needs ahead of those of her child. Nate had walked in a short time later to find Ronnie sobbing.

"My mom did treat Ronnie badly," he conceded. "But that doesn't excuse her shutting me out or leaving without a word."

"Ronnie needed to work things out on her own. She's been like that since our mom died."

"Except we both know she hasn't worked things out." And, to be honest, neither had Nate. "She's angry at me for showing up without calling ahead."

"Is that the real reason you came here? To get an answer for why she broke up with you?"

"I came to check on Samantha."

"And for closure."

"I'm over Ronnie," he insisted.

Frankie pushed off the counter. "Okay. If that's what you say."

She didn't believe him. Then again, she was hardly the only one.

Together they made quick work of the remaining dishes, both of them giving the subject of Ronnie a rest.

When they were done, Nate asked, "Are any ranches in the area hiring? Short-term, if possible. And with weekends off. This weekend, anyway. I'm going to the rodeo with Sam and Ronnie."

"I don't know of any. Spence would have a better idea. Though, you could always head into town and stop by the Poco Dinero Bar and Grill. Ranch hands regularly hang out there. Buy one of them a beer and get them talking."

It was a good idea. "Thanks for the tip," Nate said. "And for letting me park my truck and trailer. I promise not to get in the way."

"No problem."

"Dinner was great." He checked the time on his phone and grabbed his cowboy hat from where it hung on the back of the chair. "I can see myself out."

"Breakfast is at six."

"I've got food in the camper." If a couple cans of pork and beans and a box of granola bars counted as food.

"Come on, Nate. You can meet Spence."

"We'll see."

She didn't insist, and he headed out the front door to where he'd parked his truck. A drive down the main street quickly brought him to his destination, easy to find from the glowing neon signs in the window and busy parking lot.

What Frankie had predicted was true. Even on a Tuesday, the Poco Dinero boasted a fair-size crowd. Though the small stage—home to whatever band played on the weekend—was empty, a middle-aged couple shuffled across the dance floor, their steps in time to music coming from the jukebox. Small posters on each wall announced the soon to be completed recreational rodeo arena and a website for interested parties to check out the details.

Regulars sat at the polished mahogany bar, swigging their beer or whiskey, exchanging stories and occasionally checking the score of the basketball game playing on the wall-mounted TV. A second couple snuggled in the booth. A group of four men occupied a table and loudly bickered about politics and its effect on the price of cattle.

No one paid Nate much attention until he claimed the only empty stool at the bar.

His neighbor, an elderly gentleman with graying whiskers, turned and offered a friendly greeting. "A bit nippy out there."

Nate unbuttoned his jacket and slung it over the bar stool before sitting. "You can say that again."

The bartender, a small, whip-thin gal with the telltale signs of a hard life spent serving drinks either at this bar or one just like it, sidled over to take his order. Fifteen seconds later, a longneck beer was placed before him and money exchanged.

Noticing the older man's gaze returning to the basketball game, Nate said, "Suns might actually win this one."

"If their defense doesn't fall apart in the last five minutes."

He wore the clothes of a ranch hand but, from his age, Nate figured him to be retired. That didn't discount him as a source of information. In fact, he might know more than most.

"What brings you to Mustang Valley?" the man asked, lifting a glass tumbler to his lips. His hand visibly shook.

Nate was immediately reminded of his late brother, Allan, though this man almost certainly didn't suffer from cystic fibrosis. And his brother's hands had shaken only near the end and when he was especially fatigued. Yet, there was an undeniable similarity. Nate would bet money this man suffered from some health issue.

"A favor for a family friend," he answered. "But at the moment, I'm looking for work. Have you heard if any of the ranches in the area are hiring? I'm a pretty good cow wrangler. I'm also a decent handyman and have worked construction off and on."

"Check out The Small Change," the man offered. "Northeast of town. Ask for the owner, Theo McGraw. He might have an opening for a wrangler or a handyman."

"Appreciate it."

By then, the bartender sidled over. "Either of you boys ready for another round?"

Nate shook his head. "I'm good for now."

The older man raised his glass, the melting ice cubes tinkling from his shaking hand. "When you have a second, Bess."

"Coming right up, Theo."

Nate turned and stared at him. "Theo? As in Theo McGraw?"

"This here's the owner of The Small Change," Bess said. "Biggest cattle ranch in the valley."

"I do believe I've just been played." Nate tipped his bottle of beer at Theo, who grinned in return.

"The invitation to drop by still stands."

The bartender returned with Theo's drink. As if it were an afterthought, she paused to study Nate. "Do I know you?"

"I don't think so." He was often recognized by people familiar with rodeo. These days, he didn't supply his name in case someone asked what the hell had happened to his career. He didn't like admitting it had suffered a slow, painful death.

"Give me a second." She wagged a finger at him and squinted her eyes.

He attempted to distract her. "I've been here before. But it was years ago."

"Well, I'll be!" The woman beamed as recognition dawned. "You're Nate Truett."

Her announcement also got the attention of several people sitting at the bar, including Theo McGraw.

"*The* Nate Truett?" he asked.

"World champion bull rider," Bess said, bursting with pride at her accomplishment.

"Guilty as charged." Nate wished the bartender didn't have such a keen memory for faces.

"Did I hear you say you're looking for a job? Because I might have one."

"I'd be lying if I said I ever bartended."

"Oh, for heaven's sake. Not that. Something else. Something better than a wrangler. Sorry, Theo." She sent him an apologetic smile.

He laid a hand over his heart. "You wound me, dear lady."

The woman propped her arms on the bar in front of Nate. "I'll show you. On my break. Can you wait half an hour?"

"All right." Nate was intrigued.

Theo, too, judging by his expression.

Suddenly, the front door whooshed open. Along with an unwelcome gust of cold air came three people, huddled and chatting amiably. As the door banged closed behind them, they split apart. To Nate's amazement, there stood Ronnie.

The next second, she spotted him and her smile instantly died.

Chapter Three

Ronnie didn't normally swear. A ripe oath, however, slipped past her lips at the sight of Nate sitting alongside Theo McGraw, her father's boss. Luckily, her clients, the Carringtons, appeared oblivious. Not that she needed to worry. Both were former rodeo competitors and had probably heard a lot worse during their many years on the circuit.

Still, Ronnie preferred to make a good impression. Especially on clients like the Carringtons, whose daughter was one of Ronnie's students. If all went well, they'd close the deal tonight on Star Shine, a reliable beginner barrel racing horse Ronnie was selling on behalf of a friend. In exchange, she'd receive a small percentage of the final price.

A good deal for all concerned. Star Shine was an excellent match for the Carringtons' daughter and would serve her well over the next few years. The price was fair, and in return, the horse would be well cared for and doted on by the thirteen-year-old.

Hugh Carrington remained the sole holdout and had suggested they meet at the Poco Dinero to rehash the details. Ronnie had acquiesced. She and the owner, Bess, had recently entered into a business arrangement, and meeting at the honky-tonk made sense. Now, Ronnie wished she'd insisted on a different spot.

"How about that one?" Hugh motioned to an empty table near the bar, which, of course, put them in close proximity to Nate.

Ronnie sighed. Would she get even one break today? Every time she least expected it, Nate was there, insinuating himself into her life. Showing up at the ranch earlier, driving Sam home, parking his trailer at her sister's house and, now, sitting next to the man who signed her father's paychecks—both of them a pebble's toss from her important business meeting.

Hugh pulled out a chair for his wife, Jessica, and the three of them sat. Within seconds, the waitress arrived to take their order, and Ronnie indicated she'd pick up the tab when they were done.

She tried desperately to ignore Nate's stare, which burned into the side of her face, and focus on the meeting.

"The good thing about a horse like Star Shine," Ronnie said, "is that she has the ability to progress along with your daughter. You yourselves have even commented on what a good partnership they have while watching them compete together."

Jessica beamed. "I love her speckled markings."

Hugh's gaze wandered to the bar, and his ruddy brow furrowed. "Wait a sec…well, I'll be. Jessica, honey, look. Isn't that Nate Truett at the bar?"

She swiveled in her chair. "Oh, my God, you're right!"

Ronnie was thankful the pair were keeping their voices low enough that Nate couldn't hear them over the music and noise.

"We've met," Hugh commented. "Several times during my last year on the circuit. He'd just started coming up strong. Not long after that, his career skyrocketed."

"I remember," Jessica concurred.

Hugh returned his attention to Ronnie. "Does he live in Mustang Valley?"

"Passing through, I believe."

"You know him?"

For a wild second, Ronnie debated lying. "Yes," she finally admitted. "We're acquainted."

As if sensing the conversation was about him, Nate glanced their way. His brown eyes twinkling, he lifted his beer bottle in a mock toast, which Hugh and Jessica eagerly returned.

"Mind if I invite him to join us?"

Hugh didn't wait for Ronnie's reply before getting up and striding over to the bar where he and Nate engaged in a testosterone-infused reacquaintance that included a death-grip handshake and mutual shoulder clapping.

She swallowed a groan, silently begging Nate to decline the invitation. Naturally, he didn't.

At the table, he bent over Jessica for a half hug and exchange of hellos before flashing a grin at Ronnie and claiming the empty chair next to her.

"Hey, Ronnie," he said. "Hope I'm not interrupting."

She tensed but forced a smile.

"No, no," Hugh insisted, "not at all. We're thinking of buying a horse from Ronnie for our daughter. She started competing in junior events this past summer."

"If it's one of Ronnie's horses," Nate drawled, "I doubt you can go wrong."

And he would know this how?

"Actually, Star Shine belongs to a friend of mine." Ridiculous, for sure, but Ronnie felt the need to clarify. "But I've been training the horse off and on for a while."

"Like I said," Nate repeated, "I doubt you can go wrong. When it comes to barrel racing, Ronnie's a heck of a horse trainer."

She frowned. It wasn't like she needed help closing the deal. Especially from Nate.

"And teacher," Jessica added. "Our daughter adores

Ronnie. She's won three ribbons so far and is making tremendous progress."

"Isn't this past summer about the time you started your school?" Nate asked.

Technically, Ronnie had started the school this past spring, after her father had gifted her with a share of his lottery winnings. Wanting to sound more qualified, she answered, "I've been a barrel racing and Western horsemanship instructor at Powell Ranch for over three years. It's only recently I went out on my own."

There. That sounded good. And professional. She'd gotten her point across without bragging.

"What have you and your beautiful wife been up to lately?" Nate asked Hugh. "Besides having a family?"

"Working our tails off. Jessica and I own three Sandwich Nirvana shops. All of them in the Phoenix area."

"No kidding! I love your French dip."

"Me, too." Hugh grinned proudly. "It's our bestseller."

"How'd you go from rodeoing to sandwich shop entrepreneur?"

"We always wanted to own our own business. After I retired from competition, we checked into several franchises. Sandwich Nirvana was the best fit."

Hugh rambled on about his successes. Growing his first shop into three, buying a six-acre home in Mustang Valley with all the amenities, sending his children to the best private school in the area, as well as taking the family on a trip to Alaska.

Commendable, for sure, though Ronnie thought he might be going a bit overboard. Funny thing, the longer Hugh talked, the quieter Nate became.

When Hugh finally paused for air, he asked, "What about you, Nate? What have you been doing since retiring?"

"A little of everything. Traveling, primarily— mostly around the southwest. Nothing as far away as Alaska."

Hmmm, Ronnie pondered. He seemed to have a habit of giving vague answers.

"With all your talent and titles," Hugh continued, "I figured you'd be competing a lot longer than you did or moving into a related field. Didn't Rocky Mountain Rodeo Equipment make you a pretty slick offer?"

Nate twirled his bottle, watching the last of his beer slosh around in the bottom. "Unfortunately that fell through, along with a couple other deals."

"Happens sometimes. Business has its downside."

"Weren't you in some kind of accident?" Jessica scrunched her mouth in concentration. "A fall from a horse?"

That was right! How could Ronnie have forgotten? It had happened about a month after she'd left him. Mutual friends had told her Nate fell from a horse he was riding and that, though injured, he would recover. She'd been relieved and debated reaching out to him. Ultimately, she hadn't, convinced he'd reject her effort.

"Yeah," Nate admitted with a mirthless chuckle. "Seven years riding bulls, the last five professionally, and my knee was fractured by a two-year-old colt barely fourteen hands high. That's what I get for thinking I could break a green horse."

"What a shame," Hugh commiserated. "Injuries have ended more than one career. You out for good?"

"Much to my parents' and agent's disappointment." Nate's attempt at levity fell flat, as evidenced by the somber expressions of everyone at the table.

"Much to your many *fans'* disappointment," Jessica added quickly.

Hugh pointed at Nate's beer, the universal signal for inquiring if he wanted another one.

Nate shook his head. "Thanks, but I'm driving."

"I notice you aren't limping. And you're still young enough. Ever considered returning?"

"Doc told me if I injure the knee again, I might lose use of the leg for good."

Ronnie hadn't heard that part of the story.

"Which brings you to where you are today," Hugh said.

Again, Nate redirected the conversation by pointing to the posters on the wall. "What do you think about the recreational rodeo arena under construction? Instead of mechanical bulls, customers can now ride real bulls."

Ronnie observed Nate while he talked, trying to pinpoint what was different about him. The Nate from her past had been an open book. He hadn't practiced the fine art of deflection, and he certainly hadn't been mysterious.

Admittedly, she was intrigued and not because he was someone she'd once loved.

Before too long Bess came over to their table.

"Sorry to bother you folks." She smiled eagerly at Nate. "Any chance you and I can chat about that matter we discussed earlier?"

Matter? Ronnie was instantly curious.

Nate scooted back from the table, his glance encompassing the Carringtons and Ronnie. "If you don't mind…"

"Course not." Hugh shook his hand. "Hope to see you around."

Jessica wouldn't settle for anything less than a hug. "It was such a pleasure chatting with you."

"Same here."

Ronnie offered neither her hand nor a hug. She'd be

seeing him tomorrow, after all, during Sam's practice. Hating herself for it, she watched him walk away. He and Bess didn't stop at the bar, instead continuing toward the door leading out back.

"I wonder what that's about," Hugh mused.

Ronnie wondered as well but said nothing.

Eventually, she and the Carringtons returned to discussing Star Shine. Ronnie was prepared to go the distance with her pitch. It proved unnecessary.

"If Nate thinks highly of your horse training abilities," Hugh said, "that's good enough for us. We'll take Star Shine. When do you want us to pick her up?"

"When's a convenient time for you?"

Hugh wanted another drink to celebrate their deal. Thankfully, Jessica nixed the suggestion and insisted they head home.

"You ladies ready?" Hugh swept his keys and phone off the table.

Ronnie knew she should go with them; she'd parked her truck two spaces down from theirs...

"You go on. I have something to do first."

Jessica grabbed Hugh's arm and gave a little wave with her free hand. "Have a good night."

Ronnie strolled past the bar, saying a brief hello to Theo McGraw and a woman who boarded her horse at Powell Ranch. They probably assumed she was visiting the restroom. Once around the corner, she made straight for the back door, not at all sure what she'd give as an excuse if she encountered Nate and Bess.

As it turned out, she didn't need one. The tall cowboy and the tiny bartender stood at the far end of the small arena, which was brightly lit by the overhead floodlights. A bank of aluminum bleachers had been installed since

Ronnie'd last seen the arena, along with a trio of bucking chutes lined end-to-end.

Before long, the Poco Dinero would being hosting amateur bull riding and barrel racing events every weekend. When Bess had asked Ronnie to manage the barrel racing, she'd leaped at the opportunity, seeing a way to grow her school and horse training business.

As of yet, Bess hadn't found the right candidate for bull riding manager. She couldn't possibly be considering Nate, could she?

Ronnie stood in the shadows under the awning, observing him and Bess while they circled the arena. Their expressions were animated, their hands constantly making big gestures. Ronnie tried imagining other reasons for the tour. Maybe Bess was showing off her latest business endeavor to a renowned bull rider. Or, she could be seeking Nate's advice.

When they suddenly changed direction and cut across the arena, Ronnie ducked back inside rather than be caught spying. In her haste, she dropped her keys just as the door closed behind her. Murmuring her second oath for the evening, she bent to retrieve the keys. Nerves got the best of her, and she dropped them a second time.

"Shoot, shoot, shoot!"

The door banged open, missing her by an inch. She popped up, heat flooding her cheeks.

"Sorry about that? Are you okay?"

At the sound of Nate's voice, she slowly pivoted. "I, ah…" She held up her keys. "Dropped these when I went to the bathroom."

He shot a glance at the restroom door, a good fifteen feet away. "Did you?"

He clearly suspected she'd gone in search of him and

Bess. Ronnie could kick herself. Stuffing her keys in her jacket pocket, she asked, "Where's Bess?"

"Locking the equipment room."

"Okay. Well, I should skedaddle."

Skedaddle? That was the best her jumbled brain could come up with?

"Don't go yet." Nate took hold of her arm. "I have news."

She was afraid to ask, her gut insisting she wouldn't like the answer.

"Bess offered me a job. Bull riding manager. Seems I'll be staying in Mustang Valley a while longer."

Staying? And working with her? What next? Would he move into the vacant house across the street from her?

Unable to hang around and hear the rest of what he had to say, Ronnie spun and all but ran toward the door.

NATE CAUGHT UP with Ronnie halfway across the dance floor. "Hey. What are you mad about?"

She stopped abruptly, and he had to pull up fast to avoid bumping into her.

"Whoa!"

When she whirled to face him, accusation blazed in her green eyes. "No."

"No what?"

"You aren't taking the job and you're not staying in town."

He narrowed his gaze. "Last time I checked, this is a free country. I can take a job with anyone who hires me."

"You said you were heading to Houston."

"I also said my schedule's flexible."

"Why?" she demanded.

"Why am I taking the job? Honestly, I need the money."

"You do know Bess hired me to manage the barrel racing events?"

"She mentioned as much."

"And that doesn't bother you?"

"Us working together?" He shook his head. "Not especially. From what I gather, the barrel racing and bull riding events are at different times."

"Didn't you think to ask me how I felt before accepting the job?"

On closer inspection, he could see the spark in her eyes was less accusation and more…fear? Was that possible? Unlikely. But trepidation, for sure, and wariness.

"Relax, will you?" He steered her to an empty table, not the same one they'd occupied with her clients. This one was smaller. Built for two. When they sat, their knees bumped and their feet battled for the limited amount of floor space. His hand inadvertently brushed hers. Each time, her reaction was a soft intake of breath. "It's probably temporary."

"Probably?"

"We're starting with a month-long trial period."

"And what about the rodeo this weekend? You promised Sam you'd go with us. If you're working—"

"I'm going. The job's only part-time. I'll be able to work around Sam's schedule, pretty much."

"Four hours." She slumped in her chair as if every ounce of fight had drained from her. "You've been in Mustang Valley a total of four hours and already you've completely disrupted my life."

He almost chuckled and would have if she didn't look ready to cry. "Don't you think you're exaggerating?"

She raised her eyes to peer at him.

"What did I ever do to you?" He hadn't intended to raise his voice, but, frankly, he'd grown weary of her attitude. "You treat me like I was awful to you, and we both know that's not true."

"Nothing."

"I *did* nothing or you have nothing *to say*?"

She let her chin fall into her waiting hand. "You're right. I'm possibly exaggerating."

"And I repeat, why?"

"It's complicated."

Maybe so. Though, in Nate's opinion, she was using complicated as an excuse to avoid a serious discussion.

"Are you afraid of me?" he asked, his tone softer than before.

"Of course not!"

"Are you afraid of your feelings for me?"

She drew back, blinking. "I don't have feelings for you anymore."

He'd argue differently. The more he considered it, the more inclined he was to believe she wanted him gone because, like him, she wasn't over their romance. Having him close stirred too many emotions, ones she'd prefer to suppress or ignore.

"Then why do you want me gone?"

"You have a way of distracting me," she finally admitted. "I need to stay focused if I'm going to help Sam qualify for Nationals and get my new school off the ground."

"Now we're getting somewhere."

She made a face. "Don't flatter yourself."

He chose to quit while he was ahead. Ronnie had never responded well to pushing. She either clammed up, pushed back or ran away. This situation called for a different approach. One executed with finesse. Which would require him to do some explaining.

"This job is a good one for me, Ronnie, and not only

because of the money. I need something to help me get back on my feet, even if it is only temporary."

"I don't understand. Back on your feet implies you've been struggling."

He signaled the waitress and requested two soft drinks. When Ronnie didn't object, he assumed she was willing to listen and let himself relax.

"My injury didn't force me to quit competing. I lied to Hugh and Jessica."

"Then what did?"

"To borrow your excuse, it's complicated."

She didn't smile.

"Telling people I dropped out due to an injury is easier than saying I lost the drive."

"No way. You were a world champion multiple times and in multiple events. With enough drive for ten people. You can't just lose that."

"Actually, you can. Pretty easily. And not only did I lose my drive to compete, I lost my drive to do much of anything else."

She shook her head, her expression skeptical.

"What started with you dumping me and my falling out with my mother continued with my injury a month later." He took his time. Very few people knew all that Nate had been through. If he had a choice, *no one* would. "While I was home recovering from surgery, my best friend, Logan, moved to Galveston. On top of that, he picked the anniversary of Allan's death to deliver the news."

"I'm sorry."

He didn't acknowledge her apology, not quite ready to let her off the hook.

"Between losing you, my knee, not getting along with Mom, Logan moving, missing Allan, it was more than I could handle. Even after my knee healed, I stayed home. Quit competing. Avoided well-intentioned friends and family. Ignored phone calls, including the important ones. Slept a lot."

"You were depressed."

"That's too unmanly a term for a big, macho guy like me." He managed a half smile. "I prefer to say my spirits were low. After six months, my doctor recommended I get some therapy."

"Did you?"

"Naw. I loaded up Breeze and hit the road. My own personal brand of therapy."

"What happened to your sponsors?"

"Another unfortunate consequence. My agent sorted out the legalities. Ultimately, I wound up reimbursing the advances and paying the penalties for breach of contract."

Her brows rose. "That must have been expensive."

"A little." Nate had gone broke and had yet to recover. "Before I left, I sold off everything I didn't absolutely need." The one exception was the engagement ring he'd bought for Ronnie. For reasons he couldn't explain, he kept that tucked away in a drawer.

"And you've been traveling ever since?" Concern tinged her voice. For him?

"Mostly." He sat up straighter when the waitress brought their sodas and waited until she left to continue. "Allan always encouraged me to take chances. Said life's too short to live it on the sidelines. I applied that philosophy to rodeoing with pretty impressive results. Figured the same would hold true with my new lifestyle."

"I'm guessing you were wrong."

He took a swig of his soda. "I convinced myself all I needed was plenty of open highway, the occasional small town and a variety of scenery. I found odd jobs when I needed gas or food or pellets for Breeze, relaxed and enjoyed the sights when I didn't. Along the way, I met some nice people, made new friends and checked off as many bucket list items as possible."

"Did your spirits eventually lift?"

He couldn't tell if she was teasing him or not. "What's the old saying? A doctor who diagnoses himself has a fool for a patient?"

"I thought it was the attorney who represents himself has a fool for a client."

"Either way, I wasn't so much taking chances as escaping my problems. Only by then I was on a fast downward spiral and unable to stop. Not that I tried very hard." He pushed his cowboy hat back and rubbed his forehead. "I guess I needed the right incentive. Coming here, seeing what I've become though your eyes, comparing myself to Hugh—who started with less than me—I've had a rather rude awakening."

"I don't understand, Nate. You're not at all the person I knew. You excelled at rodeoing. You were, and still should be, on top of the world."

"That's the last place I want to be. It's cold and lonely up there. Hell, it's cold and lonely at the bottom."

"Is that how you felt when we were together?"

"Sometimes."

She stiffened.

"You held back, Ronnie, only trusting me with part of your heart. Which was too damn bad. I thought we had a chance for a future."

"We were young."

"That's not the reason."

Her features abruptly fell, and she averted her glance.

He reached across the table for her hand. She let him hold it, though she didn't return the gentle squeeze of his fingers. After a moment of silence, any hope he had that she'd open up and talk to him vanished.

"I'll try to stay out of your hair as much as possible," he said. "We'll only cross paths during Sam's lessons and competitions. When it comes to working together, I think we can both be civil."

She swallowed. "I want to try to get along. For Sam's sake."

"Me, too."

He released her hand, drained his soda, tossed several bills on the table and stood. "I should go. Bess strikes me as a pretty tough taskmaster, and she wants me here in the morning at nine sharp."

Ronnie also stood, though he sensed a reluctance in her to leave. Did she have more to say to him or more she wanted to hear? As always with Ronnie, she revealed very little.

He tugged on the brim of his hat. "See you tomorrow."

"Right." She took a step.

At a loud thud, followed by a low grunt and a breathy, "Oomph," they both turned. Seeing Theo McGraw in a heap on the floor beside his barstool, Nate hurried over, Ronnie right behind him.

"Mr. McGraw!" He knelt beside the man. "Are you all right, sir?"

"I'm fine, dammit."

He grabbed the older man's arm, attempting to lift him to his feet. It was no simple task. He trembled violently and had trouble putting weight on his legs.

"Leave me alone," he groused.

Again, Nate was reminded of helping his late brother, who'd given the same stubborn response when Nate had tried to lift him after a fall or out of bed. The difference was, Allan had never touched alcohol, and Theo McGraw was more than a little tipsy.

"Let me drive you home," Nate offered. Ronnie, along with several other patrons, watched his every move.

"Want me to call your ranch manager?" Bess asked. She'd scurried out from behind the bar. To Nate, she said, "He usually drops off and picks up Theo."

"I don't mind taking him." By then, Nate had managed to assist the man to his feet.

He tried to push Nate's hands away, without success. "I can get home on my own."

Bess cackled. "You can't get out the front door on your own, Theo. Let this young man drive you home. He seems capable enough."

Theo aimed his slightly unfocused gaze at Nate. "Don't think you're guaranteed a job just because you gave me a ride."

"The thought never crossed my mind." He helped the older man don his jacket. His attempt to fasten the buttons was thwarted.

After one awkward step, Theo started to sway. Ronnie pushed forward and grabbed his other arm.

His scowl dissolved into a grin. "A pretty lady. Now that's more like it."

"I'll come with you," Ronnie suggested. "You might need help getting him in and out of your truck."

In all likelihood Nate could handle Theo by himself, having had years of practice with his brother. But the prospect of her accompanying them was appealing...

"What the heck. Why not?"

Nate increased his grip on Theo's arm, and the three of them began moving slowly toward the door.

Chapter Four

How often had Ronnie ridden in the front passenger seat of Nate's truck? Too many times to count.

This truck was different, however, from the one he'd owned six years ago. For starters, it was a plain white basic model sporting several dings and scratches. The truck Ronnie recollected had been newly purchased, top of the line, and the most beautiful shade of cobalt blue. She used to check her hair and lipstick in the shiny fender when Nate wasn't looking.

He must have sold that truck to help pay off his debts and bought this one, trading luxury for economy. Well, he'd done what needed to be done, and she admired him for it. Ronnie may be doing okay for herself now, but she'd been raised in a household where money was perpetually tight and appreciated the discipline and sacrifice required to live within a budget.

That Nate should be down on his luck, after having such incredible success, was mind-boggling. And suffering from depression? All right, low spirits. Whatever he chose to call it. Imagining him being anything but positive and cheerful took effort.

A sudden eruption of loud snoring had her checking on their passenger in the rear seat at the same time Nate did. Theo McGraw's head had tipped to one side at an awkward angle. His eyes were closed, and his mouth hung wide open.

"He's asleep," she said softly to Nate.

"Sleeping it off, you mean."

"He's not supposed to drink." She shouldn't smile but did. "That doesn't stop him from sneaking out to the Poco Dinero once or twice a month when his daughter and son-in-law aren't home."

"What's wrong with him? I noticed the trembling."

"Parkinson's disease."

"I figured it was something like that."

"He's an ornery one. Refuses to follow doctor's orders. Insists on doing what he wants, when he wants. Still rides on his good days even though a fall could put him in bed for months." She pointed at the upcoming intersection. "Turn left here. The cutoff to the ranch is about a mile up the road. You can't miss it."

"I remember. Your dad took me there once when we were visiting. He's quite proud of the ranch. You'd think he owned a share."

"I suppose he is. He's worked for Theo since he and my mom first came to Mustang Valley. Thirty-five or six years ago."

"Your dad in charge of hiring the help?"

"Sometimes. He is livestock foreman. Why? You thinking of asking him for a job?"

"Theo mentioned there might be an opening."

Ronnie rolled her eyes and slumped in her seat. "Why did I not see this coming?" Nate was going to worm his way into yet another aspect of her life.

"I won't take the job if it bothers you that much."

"I thought Bess hired you."

He slowed as the cutoff came into view. "Part-time. I need to find something else. Right away, if possible. Frankie's only letting me stay at her place until Monday."

"If you think I had anything to do with that—"

"Even if you did, it's no big deal. Better I find an RV park or campground."

The main gate leading to The Small Change Ranch appeared around the next bend. Ronnie and Nate didn't talk much for the remainder of the drive. The ranch house, two stories high and bracketed by a fieldstone fence, was clearly visible in the glow from the full moon. Less visible were the stables, barns and various outbuildings situated a quarter-mile behind the impressive dwelling.

Solar ground lights lit the walkway to the front door. Nate parked in the driveway next to a late-model sedan. Theo woke up at the sound of the engine shutting off.

"What?" He lifted his head, taking in his surroundings though bleary eyes.

Nate opened his door and climbed out. "We're home, Mr. McGraw."

"When did we…oh, never mind. Doesn't much matter."

Ronnie met up with Nate just as he was assisting Theo out of the truck. She latched on to Theo's other arm right when his feet hit the ground. The older man leaned heavily against her, his breathing fast and shallow.

"Steady, now," Nate cautioned him.

Repeating the same slow walk from the bar, they progressed up the stone tile walkway to the large, ornately carved oak front door. Theo seemed to have regained a margin of his faculties during the fifteen-minute drive. Also, his mood had improved.

"Kind of you to give me a lift home."

"I was already coming this way," Nate said.

"That, young man, is a lie."

Both men chuckled. Ronnie didn't see the humor.

At the door, Theo fished first in one coat pocket and then a second for his keys, complaining loudly when he couldn't find them. He was investigating a third pocket when the front door flew open.

"Dad!" There stood Theo's daughter, Reese, dressed in a flannel robe, face freshly washed, hands planted on her hips, wearing a glower. "What are you doing? I thought you were in bed reading."

"Went for a ride."

"At this time of night?" Her gaze narrowed. "Tell me you haven't been drinking."

Theo raised his whisker-stubbled chin. "I may have indulged in a small libation. Good for the digestion."

"What will the doctor say?"

"Nothing. He's not going to find out because you're not going to tell him."

"Thank you for bringing him home." She let out a weary sigh and moved aside, allowing Ronnie and Nate to wrangle Theo up the step and over the threshold.

"We were at the Poco Dinero," Ronnie explained. When Reese looked at Nate, clearly expecting an introduction, Ronnie found herself stammering. "Th-this is my…my…" What should she call him? "My friend Nate. Nate Truett. We competed together a long time ago."

An awkward silence hung in the air, which Reese ended by saying, "Nice to meet you, Nate. I wish it was under different circumstances."

"You have a beautiful home, ma'am," he replied.

"I'll take him from here." She held out her arms. "No reason for you two to stay. It's getting late, and I'm sure you're eager to head home."

Nate and Ronnie obligingly released Theo, who swayed like a tall stalk of grass in the breeze. When Reese gripped his arm, he swatted at her hand, his temperament changing in the blink of an eye.

"Dad," she pleaded. "You're going to fall. Let me get you to your room and to bed."

"I'm not a child. I can get myself to bed."

Ronnie doubted it. Reese, too, given how she nervously fidgeted around her father.

"Let me take him," Nate said.

Reese stared, her expression startled. "I beg your pardon?"

"Hey, Mr. McGraw." Nate put a friendly arm around Theo's shoulder, smoothly taking charge of the situation. "I was wondering if I could ask your advice on a matter."

"What's that?" Suspicion clouded Theo's eyes, but he went along with Nate nonetheless.

"Have you heard about that new equine influenza outbreak?"

"No!"

"Coming this way from Texas."

"You don't say?"

As Ronnie and Reese watched, Nate escorted Theo from the living room and down the hall to where Ronnie presumed Theo's bedroom was located. Their voices grew softer, eventually dying.

"I don't believe it." Reese turned to Ronnie. "Do you think he'll be okay?"

"Your dad or Nate?"

"Both of them, I suppose."

Ronnie had to smile. "I wouldn't worry. Your dad likes Nate. They were chatting up a storm at the bar."

"Okay." Reese glanced around as if weighing her options. "You want some coffee? This could take a little while, depending on how cooperative Dad is."

"That'd be great." She could use something warm to chase away the chilly night.

Reese showed Ronnie to the kitchen, explaining that her husband was out of town on business. "Dad's quite cagey. You'd think I'd be wise to all his tricks by now. Enrico probably drove him into town. He doesn't have the nerve to refuse Dad. Not that Dad would ever fire him. Has your father ever smuggled Dad off the ranch?"

"If he has, he won't admit it."

"That's the problem." Reese motioned for Ronnie to sit. "Dad's employees are loyal to a fault. If only I could find a reliable caregiver with enough gumption to stand up to him. He scares every one of them off in a week or two. A month, if I'm lucky."

Ronnie commiserated, thanking Reese when the mug of hot coffee was placed in front of her. She helped herself to some sugar from the cut crystal bowl on the table.

The two women continued talking while they waited for Nate. Reese snuck off only once to eavesdrop on his progress and returned quickly. A half hour later, he tracked them down.

"How's Dad?" Reese asked, not hiding her concern.

"Asleep in bed."

"His meds. He's supposed to—"

"He took them. He also showered and brushed his teeth."

"Oh. Really?" She exchanged looks with Ronnie.

"Just a heads-up," Nate said. "He's not wearing his pajamas. I did convince him to put on some underwear."

"I guess I should be grateful for that much." She offered Nate a warm smile. "You're a miracle worker."

"I wouldn't go that far."

"He's been losing more and more of his abilities every day, and it's hard on him. Sneaking out to the bar is a last stand for independence." She jumped up from the table. "Would you like a cup of coffee? A sandwich? A piece of blueberry pie? Anything? I feel I should feed you in exchange for your help."

"I'm fine, ma'am. Appreciate the offer, though."

"Reese. Call me Reese. Please."

Ronnie watched the two of them, unsure what to be more amazed at. Nate's easy handling of Theo or Reese's quick acceptance of him.

Reese walked over and deposited her empty mug in the sink. "Are you in town for long?"

"A while," Nate answered.

"Hopefully, we'll see you again soon."

Ronnie interpreted that as their cue to leave and stood. Nate's next words caused her to hesitate.

"Possibly tomorrow." He flashed a wide grin. "Your father mentioned he might be hiring. Told me to drop by."

Reese brightened "Are you looking for work?"

"Something part-time. I'm not picky. Wrangler. Handyman. Laborer."

"What about caregiver? For my dad? I'd gladly pay." She named a generous hourly wage.

Ronnie stared. Had Reese really just offered him employment?

He shook his head. "Kind of you to offer, but I'm not accredited. If you ever need a hand, though, give me a call."

"I don't care that you aren't accredited," Reese said. "Or can only work part-time. Any help would be a relief."

Ronnie couldn't see Nate refusing such a heartfelt plea, but he did.

"I really can't accept, ma'am. Reese."

Her shoulders drooped, and she exhaled a long, miserable breath. Ronnie's exhale was one of relief.

"I won't take your money," he said. "But if you let me park my truck and trailer here and if there's a pasture where I can put my mare, we might have a deal."

Reese leaped forward and grabbed his hand, shaking it vigorously. "We most certainly do have a deal, Nate. Welcome to The Small Change Ranch."

Ronnie glanced away, struggling to absorb this latest, unbelievable turn of events.

BY THE TIME Nate pulled into the Poco Dinero parking lot, only three vehicles remained, including Ronnie's truck. She'd hardly spoken on the drive from the ranch. Come to think of it, she'd hardly spoken from the moment Reese and Nate had made their agreement.

"Are you okay?" he asked, stopping behind her truck and shifting into Park.

She removed her keys from the small purse she carried. Ronnie was a boots and jeans gal, except for that one accessory. She'd always adored designer purses. This particular one was glossy red with black stripes, short straps and a huge gold clasp.

Nate found her one feminine indulgence to be extremely sexy. Tough and strong on the outside, yet toting a purse straight from the shelves of a high end fashion store.

"I'm great," she grumbled as she tugged the door handle. "Just great."

"Ronnie, wait."

"What now?"

"I get you'd rather I wasn't here."

"What I want, Nate, is that you not disappoint everyone or make my life difficult." She let go of the handle in order to confront him. "Sam is my sister. Theo Mc-Graw and Reese are my father's employers. Bess is my business associate and someone I've known for years. They're important to me."

"I've been completely up-front with them about my plans and how long I intend to stay. I won't promise more than I can deliver, and I won't make your life difficult. Not if I can help it. You have my word."

"Okay. Fine. Whatever."

She automatically assumed he'd fail, which was hardly fair. He hadn't been the one to end their relationship. If anything, he'd tried to save it. And though he might have disappointed her or let her down, his actions weren't intentional.

Nate found his frustrations returning. He waited until Ronnie was halfway out the door then, unbuckling his seat belt, reached across the console and captured her arm.

She glared at his hand. "What are you doing?"

He pulled her toward him, not stopping until she was close. Very close. "I'll give you three guesses."

"Stop this. Now!" Her warm breath caressed his cheek and fire danced in her eyes, making her impossible to resist.

"Too late."

She stiffened. "I will not let—"

He ended their discussion with a swift, hard kiss.

She resisted, of course. Then again, he hadn't expected her to surrender willingly. She'd require some coaxing on his part, and Nate was up to the task. He started out by increasing his hold on her while gently moving his mouth over hers. It took some doing, but he finally got the response he wanted in the form of a tiny moan. After that, her mouth softened beneath his, and her arm slowly climbed the length of his, all the way to his neck.

At that point, he abruptly ended the kiss and pulled away. He tried not to smile.

She blinked in surprise, and then her eyes narrowed. "I don't know what game you're playing, but I won't be any part of it."

"Let's just call it a test. To see if there are any sparks."

"I can assure you, there aren't."

She was lying. He didn't call her on it, however. No point. She'd felt the crackle of desire and rush of excitement every bit as much as he had.

"We're going to talk, Ronnie. Soon. You owe me that much."

She didn't dispute him. "Sam's practice is at 2:30 sharp. Don't be late." With that, she shoved open the door and made good her escape.

Nate waited until she was inside her vehicle before leaving. Even then, he kept her in his rearview mirror until she turned onto the road taking her home. He continued to Frankie's house where he parked on the street and, as quietly as possible, crept through the gate into the backyard where his trailer was parked. After a quick check on Breeze, who appeared to be adjusting well, he headed into his trailer for a shower before climbing into bed.

Though the hour was late, he didn't immediately fall asleep. So much had happened in the span of one day, and his mind ran through each event, carefully examining them. He spent the most time dwelling on the kiss he and Ronnie had shared.

In hindsight, he should have resisted. For a multitude of reasons. High on the list, they'd hurt each other once. Terribly. Working together would be hard enough. Getting involved again was just plain stupid, what with unresolved issues the size of boulders standing between them.

When sleep finally claimed Nate, it was troubled. Rising early the next morning, he unhooked his trailer from the water hose and electrical outlet, then readied it for transport to The Small Change Ranch. Frankie's fiancé, Spence, came out and, after introducing himself, lent Nate a hand hitching the trailer to his truck.

"Tell Frankie thanks for everything," Nate said to Spence once Breeze was loaded and ready.

"Good luck. I hope things work out for you."

There was something in the other man's tone that gave Nate pause. Was he referring to the jobs Nate had landed or something else? Like, for instance, Ronnie?

He reached in his jacket pocket for his wallet. There wasn't much money in it, but he intended to compensate Frankie and Spence for his stay.

The other man held out a hand, objecting. "Your money's no good here."

"I told Frankie I'd pay rent."

"You were here overnight."

Nate sensed arguing would get him nowhere. He also sensed Spence was someone he could be friends with, if he stuck around town. "Maybe you'll let me take you and Frankie and the girls out for dinner one night."

"We'd like that."

Giving a friendly wave as he pulled out, Nate drove directly to The Small Change. Reese had sent him a text, telling him to meet Enrico, the ranch manager, at the horse stables. After settling in, he was to come to the house.

Nate hated admitting he was relieved that Enrico and not Ronnie's dad was meeting him. He and Ray Hartman had gotten along once, but that was before his botched Valentine's Day proposal and Ronnie's swift departure in the wake of it. Who knew what she'd told her father or if he'd even been informed Nate was now a fellow employee.

At the horse stables, Enrico directed Nate to drive around behind the building and park his trailer beneath a metal overhang. Nate guessed some ranch equipment had previously occupied the spot and been moved to accommodate him. He and Enrico got acquainted while Nate hooked up the trailer and unloaded Breeze.

They continued talking while Enrico led Nate and Breeze to a small pasture behind the hay shed, where the mare was introduced to a pair of older horses and a donkey. She made friends with the horses and ignored the donkey before burying her nose in the feed trough.

How much Enrico knew about Nate's employment arrangement with Reese was anybody's guess. He said nothing, though he did expound at length on the ranch and its daily operations. Nate respected the man's loyalty and discretion. Would Ronnie's dad be as loyal and discreet?

When Nate knocked on the back door to the house, Reese promptly greeted him, this time dressed for work.

"Morning!" She swung open the door. "Come in. Dad's just having breakfast. Have you eaten?"

"Not yet," he admitted before he could stop himself. The smell of bacon was just too overwhelming.

"Come. Join us."

Her enthusiastic attitude felt forced. Could be Theo wasn't exactly thrilled about the new arrangement. Nate mentally prepared himself.

The kitchen was large and shiny yet comfortable, and with all the latest appliances. Theo sat at the table, a scowl on his face.

"Dad, look who's here," Reese said. "You remember Nate from last night."

The older man grumbled and stabbed a fork into his eggs.

She smiled apologetically at Nate. "Flora will fix you anything you want." A plump, middle-aged woman in a uniform and apron appeared beside her.

"I'm not picky," Nate said. "Please don't go to any trouble."

"No trouble." Reese continued infusing her voice with false cheer.

"Whatever Mr. McGraw's having is fine with me."

Flora nodded and busied herself at the stove.

"I should leave for the work." Reese chewed her lower lip.

"Don't worry, we'll be fine," Nate assured her. He'd heard this morning from Spence that Reese was manager of the local bank.

"I left a list of instructions on the counter," she said. "Call if you have any questions."

Nate smiled at Theo. "We'll be fine."

"I know you have to be at the Poco Dinero later this morning." She reached for her briefcase. "Just stay as long as you can." Walking to the table, she bent and gave her father a kiss on the top of the head. "Be good. Please."

"You don't need to remind me."

"I love you." With a sigh, she left through the door.

"Mind if I have some coffee?" Nate asked Theo once they were alone.

"Pot's on the counter."

Nate went over and helped himself to a mug from the rack, liking that the McGraws used a drip coffee maker and not one of those modern contraptions with the little plastic cups.

When he rejoined Theo at the table, Flora set a plate of scrambled eggs, bacon and toast in front of him. He thanked her, and she melted away, probably having received instructions from Reese to leave Nate and Theo alone while they got acquainted.

"Don't think just because you drove me home last night I'm okay with you being my new prison guard."

Nate bit into a piece of generously buttered toast. "I'm not your guard, Mr. McGraw. I'd like to be your friend."

"A friend who just happens to help me on and off the toilet."

"Reese didn't mention that." Nate feigned surprise and shock. "I might have to reconsider."

"Not funny."

"You're a lucky man, Mr. McGraw. You live at home with a daughter who loves you and has the patience of a saint, and a son-in-law who doesn't consider you a burden. That's a damn sight better than residing in a nursing facility."

"I'd never tolerate that. This house, this entire ranch, is mine. I won't leave until the day they carry me out of here."

"Good. I like having job security."

He grumbled and pushed away his mostly finished breakfast, his hand shaking more than it had last night. Could be anger, Nate thought, or he was a bit hungover.

"Come on, admit it." Nate shoveled a forkful of eggs into his mouth. "I'm a damn sight better than some of your other caregivers. I can guarantee, I won't baby you."

"I get enough of that from Reese."

He probably did. She clearly adored her father and wanted only the best for him. Without meaning to, she might be micromanaging him. Nate had learned from his brother the importance, even necessity, of allowing the individual some degree of independence.

"I have an idea." He drained his coffee mug. "I'm meeting Bess at nine to start learning the ropes. I'm her new manager for the recreational bull riding, in case you didn't know."

Theo's answer was an interested lift of his bushy gray brows.

"That's less than two hours from now," Nate continued. "If you're ready by then, dressed, shaved, pearly whites brushed, you can come with me. Or, you can stay home. The choice is yours."

"Come with you?" Theo's tone was ripe with suspicion.

"Sure. Unless you think your daughter will mind."

"It's not her decision."

Nonetheless, Nate would let Reese know. And if she objected, he'd devise a plan B.

Chewing on a bite of bacon, he asked, "Well? Time's a wastin'."

Theo awkwardly pushed back from the table. "Don't think you're picking out my clothes for me, young man."

"Just as well. My taste in clothes is lacking."

Feeling rather pleased with himself, Nate finished his breakfast while Theo made his way to his bedroom. So far, his second day in Mustang Valley was getting off to a great start.

Chapter Five

"Friday and Saturday nights are reserved for bull riding,"
Bess said, "starting at seven. Barrel racing is Saturday
afternoons from two to four."

She, Nate and Theo stood at the arena fence behind the
Poco Dinero, going over precisely how the recreational
rodeo events would work.

Nate had heard of this growing sport, open to retired
professionals and amateurs alike, but hadn't actually been
to an event. He had a lot to learn.

"The Lost Dutchman Rodeo Company in Apache
Junction is the closest place for us to rent bulls," Bess
continued. "They have a good reputation and are offering
a fair price if we sign a six-month contract. The owner's
been here to see our setup, but I'd like an inspection of
his bulls before I agree."

She rolled a lollipop from one side of her mouth to
the other while she talked. Nate pegged her as a former
smoker and the habit a leftover from when she'd quit.

"That's where you come in," she told him. "I figure
you've been around bulls enough to recognize quality
bucking stock when you see it."

"I can drive over there tomorrow morning, if you
want."

"I have the owner's name and number in my office.
He seems like a decent fellow."

"He's very reputable," Theo concurred. "Been in the
business a long time."

Bess nodded at him. "That's good to know."

Nate had explained the caregiver situation when he'd arrived. She hadn't minded at all that he'd brought Theo with him or seemed worried Nate's other duties would interfere with his work for her. She and Theo both commented on their long-standing friendship, which might account in part for her understanding. He not only was a favorite customer of hers, they belonged to the same local business owners association.

Nate and Theo had been at the saloon for over two hours. There'd been paperwork for Nate to complete, a lengthy briefing of how the recreational bull riding and barrel racing events would operate, an introduction to Bess's assistant manager, Elena, who would also be helping Nate and Ronnie, a more in-depth tour of the facility and, lastly, an examination of the equipment.

Bess had asked lots of questions, seeking Nate's opinion on almost everything. He was flattered and determined not to disappoint her. During a few minutes when Theo was otherwise occupied, Nate and Bess had discussed his wages and the job's perks.

She added the promise of a raise if all went well and a gas allowance for any trips he made, including the one tomorrow to Apache Junction. She was agreeable with him taking off the next two weekends in order to accompany Sam to her rodeos, but he needed to be available every Thursday through Sunday after that. Best of all, she offered him a small advance on his pay, going so far as insisting when he turned her down.

It was a good feeling, being gainfully employed and having a roof over his head, even if that roof was the living quarters in his horse trailer.

Nate cautioned himself not to become complacent. Things could—and had—drastically changed, and without much warning.

About the time he and Bess finished up, Nate noticed Theo getting tired, though he insisted he was raring to go. He'd done a lot of walking today for someone who should be using a cane but refused.

"We'd better hit the road," Nate suggested after Bess handed him gas money and had him sign a receipt. "I'll check in with you tomorrow before I leave."

She smiled, deepening the many wrinkles on her face. "I think I'm going to enjoy working with you, Nate."

"The feeling's mutual."

He didn't tell Theo about meeting Ronnie for Sam's barrel racing practice, certain the older man would ask to go with him. His painfully slow movements screamed fatigue, and he needed to rest, whether he wanted to or not.

At home, Flora prepared them both a light lunch. Nate pretended to have an interest in some breaking news. When they were done eating, Theo invited Nate to the family room where they turned on the TV. Within minutes after sitting in his recliner, Theo nodded off, and Nate left.

He called Reese while driving to Powell Ranch and reported in. She'd been a little reluctant to let her father accompany Nate that morning. When she heard how well the outing went, relief flooded her voice.

"He'll be talking about this for weeks."

"Do you need me to come back tonight?" Nate asked. "Help him get ready for bed?"

"Gabe will be home this afternoon. I think the two of us can manage. But we have plans for tomorrow evening. If you could watch him…"

"No problem. Happy to do it." Nate likely wouldn't be getting much sleep, what with himself, Ronnie and Sam leaving at 6:00 a.m. for the Kingman rodeo. "Don't forget, I'll be gone this weekend. But if Sam places high enough, I won't need any more time off."

"No worries."

They discussed the trip to Apache Junction and whether or not Theo would go along.

"Let's wait to see how he is in the morning," Reese said. "Parkinson's is day-to-day."

So was cystic fibrosis.

Powell Ranch was busier than Nate had expected. Only while he was walking from the parking area to the barrel racing arena did he learn the reason. According to a nearby chatty couple, the huge golf tournament in north Scottsdale had drawn a flood of tourists to town and guided trail rides were going out every hour.

Nate wandered over to the bleachers and took a seat in the second row. Spotting Sam astride Ronnie's horse, waiting for her turn at a practice run, he waved. She shouted something at him that sounded like, "Watch this!"

His gaze traveled the immediate vicinity, searching for Ronnie. He didn't see her anywhere, which struck him as odd. Shouldn't she be observing Sam when her turn came?

A young woman on a strikingly marked paint gelding burst into the arena for her run. The horse might be eye-catching, Nate decided, but he was sluggish. Worse, they knocked over the last barrel. One of the helpers, an older kid of twelve or thirteen, hurried over to lift and reposition the barrel.

Nate half expected Sam to come galloping into the arena next. Instead, another rider on a dark bay did. His heart recognized her a microsecond before his brain did. Ronnie!

She flew around the first barrel, her blond ponytail

streaming out behind her from underneath her cowboy hat. Whatever cues she gave the horse were so subtle, so precise, they were barely noticeable. Yet, the horse responded instantly, his long legs a blur. While rounding the second barrel, horse and rider leaned into the turn at such a sharp angle, Nate swore Ronnie could reach down and touch the ground with her fingertips if she tried.

She cut the turn a hair too close on the third barrel, and it wobbled precariously for several seconds. Nate didn't release his breath until the barrel settled into place. No penalty for that.

Finishing her near perfect run, she urged the horse for all he was worth, and they sped past the electric timer. A scattering of applause erupted as she slowed the heavily breathing horse to a trot.

"That's how it's done," a woman near Nate commented.

He had to agree. Ronnie was spectacular, six years ago and now. The rush of emotions he'd always experienced when watching her filled his chest. Part pride. Part amazement. Part appreciation. Part love.

Wait. Not that last one. He was simply sliding into old habits, though he surely did admire her abilities. Yes, and her form.

She looked good in the saddle. Slim, athletic, graceful and confident. Oh, hell, she'd looked good all the time, including when she first woke up in the morning. He'd liked her best with mussed hair, a rumpled night shirt and sleepy eyes. Mostly because she'd reminded him of their night together. Her warm and giving body snuggled next to him. His arm draped over her waist. The scent of her soft skin when he pressed his face into her neck…

At the familiar stirring in his middle, he banished the memories. Recalling intimate moments with Ronnie would serve no purpose. Hadn't he already learned that lesson the hard way during the last six years?

Another rider entered the arena and took her run at the barrels. Nate could see Sam readying for her turn, taking her place on deck. By the time the other rider finished, Sam was in position.

"She looked good when she was warming up earlier."

Startled, Nate turned sideways as Ronnie sat down beside him on the bleachers. Worried she'd hear his heart's sudden pounding, he scooted over to give her more space.

"Yeah?" Could he come up with a lamer response? "Where's your horse?" That was almost as bad.

"Another student is cooling him down for me. She'll be giving him a go here shortly."

"I figured you'd be watching Sam's run from behind the gate."

"I want you to look at something."

"The late cue to change leads we talked about yesterday?"

Ronnie shook her head. "There's more. Watch her hands."

She'd barely finished speaking when Sam came charging into the arena on Comanche. While not quite as impressive a run as Ronnie's, the teenager did well. At least, she started out well. Nate kept his attention glued to her hands. After she rounded the last barrel, Sam took her right hand off the saddle horn, pushing the horse to even greater speed. It was then he saw what Ronnie was talking about.

"She's tugging on the reins."

"I thought so, too."

"It's slight," he said, "but enough to confuse the horse."

"You mind being the one to broach the subject? I think

she'll be more receptive to you. She and I have been having trouble communicating recently."

"Why is that?"

Ronnie shrugged. "I don't know. Maybe I'm harder on her than my other students. Maybe she's less willing to listen to me because I'm her older sister and didn't initially welcome her with open arms."

"But that changed, right?"

"Sure. Of course. In the end, Sam is family. Doesn't make reconciling with our past any easier. We're mostly on solid ground now, despite the occasional rough patch."

"Don't forget, she's still on the outs with her mom. They were extremely close until Sam learned she'd been lied to her entire life about Ray being her father. And because she and her mom are fighting, Sam hasn't seen her adoptive dad and two younger brothers in almost six months. That's a lot for someone her age to deal with."

"Believe me," Ronnie said, "I understand being on the outs with a parent. Dad and I have had our share of difficulties."

Like when Ronnie learned he'd had a child with another woman and never mentioned it? That would be enough to test the best of relationships.

"Sam's also stressed over Nationals," he added. "She gets that way before a big competition."

"And I'm stressed trying to see she finals." Ronnie rubbed a temple as if it throbbed.

"If it's any consolation, you looked as good as ever when you took your run before. Sam couldn't have a better teacher."

"Thanks." She actually sounded appreciative. "And while we're in the mood for compliments, you were really good with Theo last night."

"It's hard for a man like him to depend on others.

Allan was the same way. I figured it was better to treat Theo as a friend rather than acting like a caregiver or a nurse."

"I've never seen that side of you before. Then again, I didn't know you when your brother was alive." Her voice softened, as did her entire demeanor. "I'm impressed, Nate. More so I think than when you were winning titles."

"Tell me more." He took advantage of the change in her to inch a little closer.

She glanced up, and their gazes connected. Held. Ignited. She seemed to be searching his face for some answer. To what? Unable to resist the strong pull, he dipped his head.

And, like that, she withdrew. "Doesn't change the fact we shouldn't have kissed last night."

Okay. Shot down. Quickly and thoroughly and not unexpectedly.

Nate attempted to brush off the incident by making light of it. "Can't blame a guy for trying."

"What about this morning? How'd it go?" She was all business again.

"Oh, you know. Theo put up a fight at first. His pride insisted on that. I wound up taking him with me to the Poco Dinero, which he seemed to enjoy."

"And that went well? For you, not Theo."

"Bess officially offered me the job."

"I see." She glanced away, her eyes tracking the next rider and horse as they executed their run.

"We're both adults, Ronnie. We can work together. If you recall, we were once a pretty good team."

"That was different. And a long time ago." Her jaw tightened, signaling the end of any personal discussion.

Nate sat back, satisfied with the knowledge she still cared, whether she admitted it or not. Though what good that would do either of them remained to be seen. It could, now that he thought about it, make spending time together even harder for both of them.

"I NEED TO sign in." Sam glanced anxiously about as she hastily gathered her long blond hair into a ponytail. "My event starts in less than an hour."

"Go on," Ronnie told her, thinking how often she'd done the same thing with her hair and at the same speed. "Nate and I will get Comanche ready."

They'd parked in the large dirt lot reserved for competitors and quickly unloaded Ronnie's horse. While waiting on Nate, who'd had to park his truck in the public lot on the opposite side of the fairgrounds, they'd wiped down Sam's saddle, bridle and boots until the leather gleamed.

"What if I don't have time to warm up first?" Sam lamented.

"Standing around here won't help." Ronnie pointed in the direction of the rodeo arena. "Hurry. I'll lay out your clothes."

Honestly. Teenagers. Always requiring a swift push in the right direction.

They'd arrived late in Kingman for the rodeo. Though they'd left Mustang Valley early enough, an unexpected detour from a hazardous material spill on the highway had added almost two hours to their drive time.

Finally, Sam hurried off in search of the registration booth. Her event was scheduled immediately following the lunch break and entertainment portion of the rodeo. Less than an hour away. No wonder she was frazzled.

Ronnie had been like that, too, back when she competed. And this was an important rodeo for Sam. If she placed high enough, she'd qualify for Nationals and could skip next weekend's rodeo. A lot lay on the line.

Ronnie gave Comanche an affectionate pat. "You can do it, pal. I'm counting on you. Get her to Nationals, and we just might find you a buyer."

Sam hadn't been entirely wrong about Ronnie's motives when it came to using Comanche. She had the chance to make a tidy profit on the horse if she could add more wins to his record. That didn't alter the fact that Sam's horse was nowhere near ready to use, not without risk of reinjuring his leg.

"What can I do?" Nate's voice distracted Ronnie, and she turned to see his tall, wide-shouldered frame striding toward her.

Catching the breath that almost escaped, she asked, "You mind brushing him down while I repair his mane and tail?"

He answered her by reaching for the brush.

The previous evening, Sam had painstakingly braided Comanche's mane and tail, interweaving blue and red ribbons. During the long ride, several braids and ribbons had come loose. Ronnie used a small step stool to provide enough height that she could reach the top of Comanche's mane. As she looked down at Nate, now busily cleaning the horse's hooves with a pick and washrag, she was instantly thrown back in time.

He'd always been there for her, she recalled. Even at their worst, when they were arguing about whether or not she should compete that last time right before her miscarriage, he'd been at her side.

Stop! she told herself. One little kiss from Nate was no reason to race headlong down memory lane.

Well, not such a little kiss. She'd definitely felt the sparks, as Nate had annoyingly pointed out.

Oh, hell, she'd felt the sparks three days ago when he'd strolled out of nowhere and back into her life.

"What next?"

Nate's question derailed her thoughts, for which she was grateful. Hopping down from the step stool, she placed a hand on Comanche's neck for balance. "Let's saddle him up."

They worked together as easily and efficiently as always, right down to the small talk.

"How are early sign-ups coming for your barrel racing event?"

"Not bad." She secured a braid before moving on to the next. "Most are my students. A handful are recently retired from the circuit. There's one or two brave amateurs, I noticed."

"Are you going to enter?"

She laughed. "Even if it wasn't against the rules, I'd pass."

"Why? I watched your run the other day. You could return to competing no problem."

"I'm too old."

"Wasn't there some woman who recently earned a title at fifty-nine?"

"Yes." Ronnie had heard of her, as had almost everyone in the rodeo world. "But I'm happy teaching and running the event at the Poco Dinero."

"Have you competed at all since…" He didn't finish.

"No."

After the reference to their unhappy past, neither of them spoke again. They were polishing the silver conchos and accents on Sam's saddle when the teenager returned.

With a quick, "I've got to get ready," she scurried past them and climbed into Ronnie's camper.

Kingman's Andy Devine Days wasn't the biggest rodeo in the state by any means. Nonetheless, Ronnie had insisted Sam give it the same consideration as one twice the size. As a result, Sam looked every inch the professional barrel racer when she stepped out of the trailer fifteen minutes later, and Comanche was impeccably groomed from head to toe.

Ronnie gave her sister a last-minute inspection.

"Well?" Sam demanded.

"You're only missing one thing." Ronnie reached into her pocket and removed a silver horse-head pin, which she affixed to Sam's shirt collar. "For luck. Dad gave this to me on my fourteenth birthday. I wore it in every competition after that."

"Really?" Sam's entire countenance changed, and she visibly held back tears. "Thanks, Ronnie."

"You're welcome." Ronnie had to fend off her own flood of emotions.

"That was nice of you," Nate said after Sam rode off toward the practice ring.

"It was just collecting dust in my jewelry box."

Rather than press her, Nate gave her a much appreciated break while they tidied up around the trailer.

"Be back in five," she said when they were done, and disappeared inside the camper to freshen up. "Because I'm covered with dirt and horsehair" she mumbled as she washed her face and combed her hair in the tiny bathroom. "Nate has nothing to do with it."

Right. Just like he had nothing to do with her applying mascara, blush and lipstick.

"What are you doing?" she asked, evaluating her reflection in the mirror. She'd hurt him. Terribly. And had no business encouraging him. When he'd kissed her the other night, she should have immediately pushed him away and insisted they not let that happen again. Instead, she'd responded and most certainly given him the wrong idea.

His appreciative glance when she stepped out of the camper lingered. "Wow. You look great!"

"I want to be ready in case I meet any potential clients."

The explanation satisfied her. The twinkle in Nate's eyes said he thought some of her efforts were for his benefit.

He was wrong, of course. *So very wrong.* She lifted her chin a notch and purposely faced away from him as if searching for someone. His deep chuckle infuriated her. She didn't like him guessing what she was thinking.

They walked side by side to the warm-up arena, planning to watch Sam before she competed. Ronnie carefully maintained a good six inches of space between them at all times, refusing to dwell on his confident walk, strong profile and how the breeze teased the dark hair peeking out from beneath his cowboy hat.

She cleared her throat. "Did you have a chance to talk to Sam about her pulling back on the reins?"

"Yeah. When we stopped for gas this morning. You were inside the mini-mart buying coffee. I figured she'd be more receptive if you weren't around."

Ronnie wasn't offended. Mostly because he was right. "And?"

"It went fine."

The crowd grew denser once they left the parking lot and entered the arena grounds. White tents lined both sides, food to their left, merchandise and services to their right. The setup created a long aisle leading to the main arena.

During the walk, they were assaulted by the delicious aromas of fry bread and barbecue and kettle corn. A vendor selling colorful fringed vests caught Ronnie's attention, and she decided to return later for a closer inspection.

"Sam was receptive then?"

"Pretty receptive," Nate said. "We'll see when it's her turn."

"But she agreed she was pulling back on the reins?"

"Not exactly, though she didn't disagree."

Ronnie could have predicted as much.

"What are your plans for the riding school?"

His question took her momentarily aback. "Plans? Besides doubling the number of students, training the best barrel racing horses in the state and becoming wealthy beyond my wildest dreams?"

"I see you have no small ambitions."

She almost laughed. He could be charming and endearing when he chose, and she'd have to watch herself. "Truthfully? Make a decent living and have a good, no, *a great*, reputation."

"You've done really well for yourself, Ronnie."

The warmth and sincerity in his tone flattered her. "Thank you."

"I'm not sure you'd have accomplished as much if we'd stayed together."

She stopped midstep. "Why do you say that?"

"I put my career ahead of yours."

"I'm not sure you did. But, in all fairness, you had the better career."

"Doesn't make what I did right."

"Water under the bridge." She took a step.

"Is it?" He stopped her with a hand on her arm. "Both our lives were completely changed that day."

Which day was that? she mused. When she'd miscarried? His wrecked Valentine's Day proposal? The day she'd walked out without telling him?

"Yes." Ronnie forced herself to breathe evenly. She really did owe him an explanation.

Not now, however, and when she started forward a second time, he let her go. Relief flowed through her, allowing her pulse to slow its beating.

The crowd at this rodeo looked pretty much like those at every other one. The various groups were easy to spot. Spectators, competitors and their family and friends, rodeo workers, and those in the business—trainers, horse traders, and equipment or supply merchants. Some, Ronnie included, fell into more than one category.

As expected, they encountered several familiar faces, frequently pausing for a brief hello. Nate, Ronnie noted, was always greeted warmly despite his lengthy absence from competition. When asked what he was up to, he answered bull riding manager for the Poco Dinero, which seemed to interest a great many folks.

He also made each statement with a small amount of obvious pleasure, if not pride. A big change from his first day in Mustang Valley a few days ago, when he'd seemed subdued and reserved.

What had he told her in the bar? That he needed the job and not just for the money? Hadn't she herself learned the importance of pride in one's accomplishments?

At last, she and Nate reached the warm-up ring, where they immediately spotted Sam and Comanche. Rather than trotting or loping the horse in order to loosen his muscles, Comanche stood in place while Sam carried on an animated conversation with a friend Ronnie recognized.

She wanted to shout at Sam to quit wasting time and get a move on. Biting her lower lip, she suppressed the urge.

Fortunately for them both, Sam spotted Ronnie and

gently nudged Comanche with her heels. Leaving her friend behind, she began putting the horse though his warm-up paces. Ronnie sighed expansively.

"You okay?"

She sensed Nate's stare on her and purposely lightened her voice. "Couldn't be better."

Soon after that, the announcement came that the barrel racing event was starting. Because Sam had been late registering, she'd be the last to go. They agreed Nate would remain with Sam while Ronnie went ahead to the arena and checked on the competition.

There were several impressive runs, Ronnie decided, but none Sam couldn't beat. She hoped Nate was offering Sam advice and that the teenager was listening for a change. Eventually, Ronnie spotted them in the area behind the gate where Sam would wait for her turn. She rushed over to join them, skirting around horses and riders and spectators.

As with every similar situation, Ronnie briefly flashed on the day she'd fallen after nearly being trampled by the runaway horse. Automatically, she looked in all directions, making sure the coast was clear. Emotions rose inside her, a fresh attack of grief and guilt and sorrow. She ruthlessly held them at bay.

"Four more competitors to go," she said as she neared, feeling more in control.

Sam straightened in the saddle. Both she and Comanche appeared ready.

"You've got this," Nate told her. "Just remember to cue his lead change the second you come out of the pocket and watch that right hand."

"I got it." Sam's terse response could be, and probably was, the result of nerves.

Ronnie gave a start when Sam's name was called.

"She'll be great," Nate assured her and led her to a spot on the fence where they'd have a better view of Sam's run.

"Good luck!" Ronnie hollered.

Sam reached a hand up and touched the silver horse-head pin. Seeing that caused a small lump to form in Ronnie's throat. Whatever differences they had, Sam was her sister, and they'd come to love each other.

Six inches of separation weren't possible at the fence, not with the crowd squeezing in. Ronnie and Nate stood touching from the shoulders down. She tried ignoring the warmth radiating from him and the firm pressure of his body against hers.

That was until the moment Sam and Comanche entered the arena at a full gallop, his hooves flying and her head low as she leaned forward over the saddle. Then, Ronnie's attention was entirely focused on Sam.

"You got this," she murmured under her breath, every muscle in her body rigid.

"Come on," Nate said between clenched teeth.

Sam's run, over in the blink of an eye, was almost flawless. Nate whipped his hat off and, whooping loudly, waved it in the air above his head. Ronnie hollered, "Good ride!" as Sam sped past them out of the arena. When Sam's results were posted on the jumbotron, Ronnie couldn't help herself and let out a yelp. "Second place!"

Nate's grin spread from ear to ear as his arm slipped around her waist. "She's advancing to the final round tomorrow."

Without a conscious thought, Ronnie turned into him, pulled his head down to her level and planted a kiss on his cheek.

He increased his hold on her and whispered low and sexy, "Don't stop there, sweetheart."

Chapter Six

After the first twenty miles of Sam's nonstop chatter, Nate had begun blocking her out. That had been a hundred-and-seventy miles ago. She hadn't taken a break in all that time. It was a wonder her phone hadn't died. Fifteen more miles and they'd reach home.

Since when did he think of Mustang Valley as home? With all the traveling he'd done and long-ago move from Abilene, he didn't call anyplace home. The thought gave him pause.

"It was incredible," Sam gushed. "Yeah, fifteen-point-ten seconds. My best time in I don't know how long. The entire crowd cheered. When I accepted my first place ribbon and buckle, the guy in the booth announced the win qualified me for Nationals."

She was describing the events from earlier—day two, and the final round of barrel racing. Nate had lost track of how many people she'd told. This call, however, was different. Sam was talking to her mom.

He couldn't tell from Sam's tone if the rift between mother and daughter had healed or simply narrowed. Sam was still riding an emotional high, which accounted for her elevated mood.

Whatever the case, he was glad she and her mom were conversing and not arguing. He recalled the first friendly phone call with his own mother after their two-year estrangement. Tomorrow he'd let her know about Sam and her mother's reconciliation, if Sam's mom didn't beat him to the punch.

Nate let himself smile. He'd accomplished what he'd set out to do, check on Sam and help if possible. Not that he intended to leave anytime soon. He liked his two new jobs and, if he said so himself, was doing pretty well at them.

Bess had been impressed with his assessment of the bulls at Lost Dutchman Livestock Company and his suggestions for renegotiating the contract terms. Reese thought he walked on water. Her description, not his. She was exaggerating, of course, but apparently his approach to caring for Theo was more successful than that of the man's previous caregivers. Perhaps because Nate sincerely liked Theo and enjoyed their hours together.

Over the din of Sam's spirited conversation, he heard his own phone go off. Grabbing it from the compartment in the console beside him—his old truck didn't have Bluetooth capabilities—he checked the display.

Ronnie's name and number appeared, sending a sudden surge of surprise and excitement through him. They'd spoken only when absolutely necessary since yesterday and her excited reaction to Sam's run. All she'd done was give him a peck on the cheek. No big deal. Nate couldn't figure out what was bothering her.

Unless it was the smoldering look they'd shared and his less than subtle suggestion she not stop there. Or her name, which he'd uttered in a soft, urgent whisper. Right next to her ear. After she'd pulled his head down to her level. Which was right after she'd leaned into him. Or, was it the other way around?

Nate hadn't dared do more. Ronnie needed to be the one to make the next move. But she hadn't. As if coming to her senses, she'd withdrawn. When Sam rode over to them moments later, it was to discover her sister and family friend eagerly waiting to congratulate her.

Answering Ronnie's call, Nate automatically checked the side mirror, noting the reflection of her headlights. She'd been behind him the entire drive from Kingman.

"Hey," he said cheerily, "is there a problem?"

"What's going on with Sam? I've been calling her for the past hour and keep getting her voice mail."

Okay. Not the least bit interested in talking to him. Well, what had he expected? A sudden outpouring of feelings? A confession that she'd been thinking about him as much as he'd been thinking about her? An invitation to finally have that long overdue talk?

"She's been on the phone," he answered. "At the moment, she's talking with her mom."

"Oh." There was a pause before Ronnie continued. "Are they being civil?"

"Downright friendly, from what I can hear."

"That's good, I guess. Right?"

"I think so."

"Well, I was going to suggest we stop at the gas station on the way into town. Sam can ride with me the rest of the way home. That would save you some extra driving."

"Sounds like a plan."

It had been Ronnie's idea for Sam to ride with Nate. He'd been admittedly baffled, assuming she'd want to share in Sam's excitement and discuss various strategies for Nationals. Maybe, possibly, Ronnie had needed some alone time to contemplate the many changes his recent appearance had wrought in her life.

"You know where it is?" she asked.

"On the south side of the road. Next to the auto parts store."

Nate stifled a yawn. It was late, and they'd had a long, grueling day that included a nearly four-hour drive.

Thinking ahead to his 7:00 a.m. shift with Theo the next morning added to his weariness.

"Sam's going to have to practice harder than ever," Ronnie said. "Local rodeos are nothing compared to Nationals. The competition is intense. Well—" she paused "—you'd know that better than anyone."

He did and wondered if she'd attended any National Finals after her miscarriage. Not Nate. He'd been invited more than once to watch friends compete. After he'd turned them down enough times, they'd stopped asking—which was fine by him.

"I'll be there to help as much as I can," he told Ronnie. "The first recreational bull riding event is next weekend."

"Bess didn't tell me."

"She called me earlier today." Actually, she'd let him know she'd signed the revised contract with Lost Dutchman. "I'm sure she'll contact you tomorrow. She probably figured you were busy with Sam."

"I suppose."

He could hear the uncertainty in her voice and attempted to reassure her. "I wouldn't worry about it."

"I'm not. And barrel racing doesn't require nearly the preparation bull riding does. Neither is it as big a draw."

Did that bother her? Nate decided no. Ronnie's entire purpose in managing the barrel racing events for Bess was to get her name as a trainer, and the name of her school, in front of as many people as possible. This wasn't a competition between them.

For that reason, Nate would do his level best to guarantee a smooth working relationship. Hadn't he and Ronnie been getting along fine when it came to Sam? Unexpected kiss and intimate exchanges aside. And with this being Sam's last rodeo of the year, they wouldn't be traveling together again.

Unless Sam insisted he accompany them to Vegas for Nationals in three weeks. Would she? They hadn't discussed the possibility. Ronnie might not welcome him. And he had his two new jobs to consider, though he imagined his employers would give him time off. The entire town was pulling for Sam, as they'd once pulled for Ronnie.

The real question was, how would he and Ronnie feel? Nationals was sure to evoke many difficult memories.

"If you need help with setting up for Saturday," he told her, "let me know. I'll be there all day."

"Um, thanks. I should be fine. I have a couple of students and their parents coming."

"Okay. See you at the gas station."

He'd only just disconnected when Sam ended the call with her mother. "That went well," he said.

"Real well." She positively beamed.

"We're meeting Ronnie at the gas station. To swap you out."

"I'm glad she suggested I ride with you and that we were able to spend time together."

Had she actually just said *spend time together*? She'd been on the phone the entire drive.

Nonetheless he agreed. Why burst her bubble? "Me, too."

At the gas station, Nate got out and walked Sam to Ronnie's truck. He really didn't have to, as the station was well-lighted and he could have tracked Sam's progress from his truck. Except, he'd have missed seeing Ronnie's expression of mild discomfort up close, and that was worth a short walk.

Sam was reaching for the truck door when her phone rang. Naturally, she answered it before getting in. Nate didn't pay any attention; he'd become immune to her conversations. With a goodbye salute and, "Take care," he began walking away.

"Nate," she called out. "Hold on a second. It's Frankie. She having a cookout tomorrow afternoon to celebrate my win. One o'clock. She says you're invited."

He stopped and stared back at the truck. Sam smiled expectantly. Not Ronnie.

He should decline. The rocky road they were traveling wouldn't get any easier by them spending more and more time in each other's company. Especially if that time was social in nature as opposed to business. Not to mention the potential awkwardness of being around Ronnie's family.

On the other hand, Sam was a close friend of Nate's family and, in a small way, he'd contributed to her success. Frankie wouldn't have invited him if she didn't anticipate things going well.

"I'll be there" he said, watching Ronnie's internal struggle play out on her face. "Tell Frankie thanks and ask her if there's anything I should bring."

Sam relayed the message, coming back with, "You're welcome and nothing but yourself."

"See you tomorrow." Nate returned to his truck, a spring to his step that hadn't been there when he pulled into the gas station.

He was still in a good mood the next morning when he entered the main house at seven to assist Theo with his morning routine. The older man had only just woken up and came stumbling into the kitchen, hair mussed and wearing his bathrobe.

"Morning, Mr. McGraw!" Nate held up the mug of coffee he'd poured for himself. "Want some?"

"Black and hot," Theo grumbled and dropped into a chair, palms braced on the table to help steady himself.

Sleeping late and up on the wrong side of the bed at that.

"Where's the family?" A text from Reese earlier had instructed Nate to go on in, that she and her husband were leaving early and wouldn't be there.

"A cattle sale in Cottonwood."

"Last minute?" Nate hadn't been informed of any day trip.

"If you ask me," Theo bit out, "Gabe's been planning this for months and didn't want to tell me."

Ah. That explained his grumpiness. Theo would have wanted to attend the cattle sale with them, and wasn't physically up to such a strenuous trip. They'd waited to tell him until the last minute in order to avoid a battle.

"Is Flora here?" Surely they weren't leaving Theo alone all day. Nate considered texting Reese.

"Her day off. They've recruited Enrico—it's his turn to play prison guard. Though I'm sure he'll have some excuse about needing to discuss ranch business that can't wait until tomorrow. That's how they work it, you know. They concoct these elaborate ploys, hoping I'm too stupid to see through them."

"I'm sure that's not true. You're anything but stupid, sir." Nate placed the coffee mug in front of him. "Since Flora's off, can I fix you breakfast?"

"I'm not hungry." He spoke gruffly, but Nate could see the sorrow and disappointment in his eyes.

"All right. Suit yourself."

Rather than chide the older man or lecture him about keeping up his strength, Nate found a package of bagels in the bread basket and cream cheese in the refrigerator. Also a carton of orange juice.

It wasn't much. Enough, however, to gain Theo's interest. "You can throw one of those bagels in the toaster oven for me, too, while you're at it."

Nate did. He also poured a second glass of orange juice.

He truly sympathized with Theo and didn't let the man's crankiness bother him. As owner of the valley's largest cattle ranch, he'd no doubt attended sales his entire life until Parkinson's struck. Not being able to go, and having his family hide their trip from him on top of that, must really hurt.

Then again, Nate understood why Reese and her husband had chosen to semi-sneak away. Arguments like the one that might have ensued could be draining, frustrating and counterproductive. Theo's condition didn't stop the ranch from needing to be run. Reese and her husband were doing the best they could under trying circumstances.

"You ready to hit the shower?" Nate asked when he and Theo finished their breakfast. They'd eaten in almost complete silence.

"I don't need a shower."

"Okay. Then, let's get you shaved and dressed."

"I'm going to skip shaving today, and I can dress myself. Or, maybe I'll wear my pajamas all day, seeing as I'm housebound."

"All right." Nate went about clearing their few dishes and loading them into the dishwasher. "I'll keep you company until Enrico arrives. At least tell me you've taken your meds."

Theo's answer was to frown.

"I'll get them for you."

His balled fist hit the table with a loud smack. "I don't need a damn babysitter."

Nate sat down beside him. "No, sir, you don't."

"I have half a mind to fire you."

"You could. There's nothing stopping you. But your daughter will just hire another caregiver. You know that. And he or she probably won't take you to the bull riding event at the Poco Dinero this coming weekend."

"You're trying to bribe me."

"Not really." Nate grinned. "Okay, I am. A little."

Theo grumbled again, this time with less anger.

"You go ahead and lash out at me all you want if it makes you feel better. I'm pretty tough, and I can take it. Spent a lot of years helping my brother with whatever he needed, including letting him vent. Mostly he yelled. Sometimes, he laid into me." Nate rubbed his chin as if it ached. "Had a pretty good right hook for someone with cystic fibrosis."

Theo studied him at length. "You don't talk much about him."

"They don't come any better than Allan. Taught me a lot. I could tell you some stories while you're getting dressed."

With considerable effort, Theo pushed to his feet. "I suppose I could listen."

It was, Nate realized, the closest he was going to get to an apology.

NATE'S MOTHER HAD taught him to never show up at someone's house for dinner empty-handed. Since Frankie had said there was nothing he could bring, he settled on fresh-cut flowers from the local market. At the last minute, he'd selected a second bouquet for Sam, to celebrate her win and upcoming trip to Vegas.

"Why, thank you," Frankie gushed when he handed her the flowers.

Sam had answered the door when Nate arrived. As a

result, she was already showing off her bouquet. Most notably, to a young man about her age. A boyfriend? She'd mentioned going out on dates when comparing herself to Ronnie, who *didn't* go out.

Should Nate be worried? About Sam, not Ronnie. Report back to his mom so that she might inform her best friend? He decided to get to know the guy first. Besides, he didn't look like Sam's type. Nate would have expected to see Sam with one of the local wranglers or the son of a rancher. Boots, jeans, cowboy hat, impeccable manners. This guy wore scruffy sneakers and a *Star Wars* T-shirt. His unruly hair kept falling in front of his black glasses and blocking his vision, at which point he'd flick his head.

Where in the heck had she met him? Certainly not at a rodeo.

"You know Spence and the twins already," Frankie said. "And Mel, of course."

Yes. Ronnie's other sister. Noticeably pregnant and looking far different from the last time they'd met. He shook her hand. "Good to see you again. And congratulations."

"Of course, you and Dad are already acquainted." Frankie then introduced Nate to the rest of the guests.

They included Mel's husband, who happened to be the town deputy, and his young daughter. Also present were Ray's new wife, Dolores, several of the Hartmans' other friends, and a few of Ronnie's students.

Ronnie, herself, seemed to be avoiding him. What the heck was she afraid of? That he'd haul her off and kiss her again. That *she'd* kiss *him*?

Truly, she was being silly. He'd promised to not cause her any trouble and wouldn't. Certainly not while they were in the company of two dozen people.

"How 'bout a beer?" The question came from Ray Hartman.

Nate thought a beer might be just what the doctor ordered. "Sure thing."

"The ice chests are on the patio." Ray led Nate across the family room and outside.

Half the guests had spilled onto the patio, taking advantage of the beautiful day. Late fall in central Arizona could be chilly. It could just as often be warm and balmy. Add a clear blue sky to the elevated temperature, and it was a recipe for perfect cookout weather.

Ray lifted the lid of an ice chest tucked against the exterior wall and removed two beers. He passed one to Nate. "I hear things are going well with Theo."

"Wish I'd known him before the Parkinson's. He must have been pretty imposing."

Ray chuckled. "Still is."

They talked companionably for several minutes, mostly about Theo, the ranch and Sam's win. Nate was reminded of how much he'd once liked Ray, and was relieved to sense no hard feelings about what happened between him and Ronnie years ago. That was until Ray abruptly changed the subject.

"I've always regretted not having the chance to talk to you after…well, you know. Ronnie's mishap. She asked me not to. Then the two of you…" He faltered once more. "A real shame."

"I appreciate that, Ray."

"It can be hard on the whole family when a couple calls it quits."

Nate didn't correct him by pointing out that Ronnie had been the one to leave him and the decision was hardly mutual.

"I really thought you both had what it took for the long haul."

"Apparently not."

"Glad to see you're getting along now. Can't be easy."

Nate's gaze found Ronnie. She'd carried out a platter of hamburger patties and one of hot dogs to Spence, who was in charge of the grill.

"We broke up a long time ago. No reason not to get along."

"Well, it's clear you've both moved on."

Was it? Then why did Nate feel the same old irresistible pull toward Ronnie? It was more than her hair—which she'd left unbound for a change to tumble down her back like water over a cliff—though, damn, he'd loved running his fingers through it and had frequently.

Neither was it her dressy blouse, a change from the standard western-cut work shirt she typically wore. This top had a snug waist, deep V neck and flowing sleeves that emphasized her knockout curves. Curves he'd spent considerable time learning their various shapes.

Memories. Moments. Shared experiences. A once profound connection. A heart with a big hole in it. Those were the things that called to Nate and compelled him to glance her way every minute or two.

He confessed to liking her new and different look, and he wasn't the only one. Numerous admiring glances had been cast in her direction by the men there. Even Sam's goofy boyfriend had stared at Ronnie as she'd strolled by him with the platters. Apparently he was less of a nerd than Nate had first thought.

"Too bad about the miscarriage," Ray said. "I'm not sure Ronnie ever got over that."

The remark had Nate redirecting his attention. "I doubt anyone does."

"It wasn't her fault."

"Is that what she said?" Nate took a swallow of his beer, noting that while several people stood in close proximity, none of them appeared to be listening in. "Did she tell you I blamed her?"

"Not at all!" Ray was quick to set the record straight.

"Because it isn't true."

"She blames herself. Only herself. I just wish she'd stop. Maybe if you…" Ray paused, his expression expectant.

"If I what?"

He cleared his throat. "Hard to say what might have happened with you and Ronnie had things gone differently. A word from you might allow her to forgive herself."

Part of Nate wanted to fire back at Ray. He'd been nothing but kind in the aftermath of his and Ronnie's tragedy. Supportive. Attentive. She, on the other hand, had pushed him away, shut him out and tossed his heart back when he'd attempted to give it to her for always.

"There isn't much I can say to her I haven't already. She was in the wrong place at the wrong time."

"She has so many regrets and has spent too much time dwelling on them."

"Did the same thing myself."

"I heard."

What all had Ray heard? Nate wasn't sure and didn't ask. This wasn't the place for a melancholy walk down memory lane.

"I've approached Ronnie twice this week," he said. "She doesn't appear inclined to have a conversation with me."

Ray expelled a long, weary breath. "She's hardheaded. Like her old man."

Nate drained a good portion of his beer. "I'll gladly talk to her, if the opportunity arises, which I doubt will happen. But I think she's going to have to work through this on her own."

"I suppose."

A family friend came over to retrieve a beer from the ice chest and say hello to Nate. He was curious about the upcoming bull riding event and asked for details. Nate welcomed the distraction.

"You coming this weekend?" he asked Ray when the man left.

Ray brightened. "Wouldn't miss it."

"You could sign up. Take a spin on one of the bulls."

That earned Nate a hearty belly laugh. "I prefer to spend my days herding bovine, not riding them."

And, like that, they resumed a friendlier, less tension-filled conversation.

Eventually Spence moseyed over to join them, having relinquished the grill to Frankie, the expert cook in their family. Nate proceeded to learn more about racing quarter horses in the next ten minutes than he had in his entire life.

"What kind of horses to you have?" Spence asked.

"Just the one. A quarter horse mare. She's old now, and retired, though we've managed nice, leisurely rides in the hills behind The Small Change. Was thinking of taking her out again this afternoon if I get home in time. It's a beautiful day."

Before long, Frankie announced the food was served. Buffet style. A line had already started forming inside at the breakfast bar.

Nate decided not to overstay his welcome. Right after the cake was served and a toast made in Sam's honor—nonalcoholic beverages for those under twenty-one—he made his made his goodbyes. He considered seeking out Ronnie, and would have if she wasn't among the group of women surrounding her sister Mel and extolling the virtues of various baby names.

"Thanks again," he told Frankie and Spence when they escorted him to the door. "I had a nice time."

Frankie gave him a hug. "I hope Dad didn't stick his nose in where it didn't belong."

"He cares about Ronnie, and I respect that." Nate would have done the same in the man's shoes.

On the short drive through town, he decided enough daylight remained he could take Breeze out for a ride—if he hurried, and if they didn't go for more than an hour. That was about all his old mare could handle anyway.

One of these days, when he had a free morning or afternoon, he'd ask Theo if he could borrow a ranch horse and go on a longer, more strenuous outing. Nate liked pushing himself and hadn't had the chance for several months, since his last visit with his parents.

Reaching his trailer at the ranch, he parked and went inside to change into his riding clothes. While riding Breeze up and down an easy trail and enjoying the desert landscape, he mentally reviewed his tasks for the upcoming week. He needed to locate at least one more horse and rider to herd the bull out of the arena after each run and another to operate the gate. With the Lost Dutchman providing wranglers to handle the bulls, Nate had one less item on his list.

He decided to ask Theo's advice. The older man had steered him in the right direction before and might know someone who fit the bill. Plenty of former rodeo hands, as well as competitors, wound up working for ranches after leaving the circuit.

Checking the time, Nate turned Breeze around and

aimed her back in the direction they'd come. A half mile outside the ranch, she quickened her pace, sensing they were almost home.

When they neared the horse stables, she suddenly lifted her head and gave a soft whinny. Nate patted her neck, assuming she was simply glad to be home and hoping for a dinner of fresh hay.

"Getting hungry, girl?"

They'd been out a bit later than Nate planned. The sun had set ten minutes ago. This time of year, dusk fell very quickly.

All at once, Breeze came to a standstill, her ears pricked forward. He looked in the direction of his trailer and saw what had the old mare's attention. His heart gave an abrupt, sharp knock.

Ronnie stood there, near the door of his living quarters, wearing the same red Arizona Cardinals hoodie he'd seen her in that first day.

Nate dismounted, his movements slow and unconcerned and in complete opposition to the tension coursing through him. Why was she here and what did she want? Holding on to the reins, he walked over to meet her, Breeze plodding along behind him.

"I wasn't expecting to see you." He intentionally kept his voice level and casual. "Waiting long?"

She shook her head. "Hope you don't mind. I… I should have called first. But I thought…"

"I'd say no?" he suggested.

"Something like that. I did kind of ignore you at the party earlier."

She slipped a small purse up the length of her arm, letting the strap rest in the crook of her elbow. This one was pink with big red hearts and Cupid's bows. Nate was instantly reminded of Valentine's Day and his proposal.

Had she chosen that particular purse on purpose? Was she remembering, too?

"Is there something you want, Ronnie?" He hitched his chin at Breeze. "I need to unsaddle her."

"I, um, was hoping we could talk."

"Really? Because you haven't wanted to talk whenever I've tried."

She had the decency to look contrite. "I'm sorry about that."

"Did your dad by chance put you up to this?"

She drew back. "My dad? No. What makes you think that?"

"He mentioned our history at the cookout." Seeing her stricken expression, he said, "Never mind. I obviously misunderstood."

"O…kay." She appeared more troubled than convinced.

He took pity on her. Tying Breeze's lead rope to a metal ring on the outside of the trailer, he proceeded to unsaddle the mare. "Is this about working together? Or did I inadvertently say the wrong thing at the cookout?"

"Not at all. Everyone likes you." She moved marginally closer, confusing him even further. "I owe you an explanation for what happened six years ago, and it's time I gave it to you."

Chapter Seven

Ronnie knew she should say something. Anything. She'd come to The Small Change, learned from the guy cleaning stalls that Nate had gone riding on Breeze, waited the twenty-plus minutes outside his trailer for him, then announced she owed him an explanation.

Only, here she was, following three steps behind him while he returned Breeze to the pasture, racking her brain for the right words and praying she wouldn't sound stupid. So far, she'd commented on the weather, Sam's practice schedule for the upcoming week and what kind of crowds they might expect at the Poco Dinero this weekend.

Gauging by his brief answers, Nate hadn't been riveted. He was obviously waiting for her to cut to the chase.

She'd never been good at expressing herself. In their last weeks together, when she'd become increasingly withdrawn, Nate had accused her of purposely shutting him out. Had she? Her sisters thought she'd inadvertently learned to hold in her emotions when their mom died. Everyone had been too immersed in their own grief and despair to listen to a young child.

The loud clang when Nate shoved the gate latch into place gave Ronnie a start, and she jerked.

"Nervous?" he asked, his gaze boring into her.

He would have to notice her reaction.

"No, no. I, ah, stepped in a hole."

"Be careful." His lazy drawl became even lazier. "There are a lot of…holes…around here."

Dammit, he knew she was lying. He'd always been much too adept at reading her.

"You want to go somewhere else?" he asked.

"What?" She blinked.

"You seem uncomfortable. We could go to the bar. Or, the café for coffee."

"No." She shoved her hands in her hoodie pockets. "This is just harder than I thought it would be."

"Why did you come if you're not ready to talk?"

"You being at Frankie's today, chatting all cozy-like with Dad and the rest of my family, joking with Sam's friend...it seemed, I don't know, easy and natural. As if you belonged." She raised her eyes to his. "I realized you did belong at one time, and I took that away from you."

"I like your family. I'd forgotten how much fun big gatherings are."

That surprised her. "Don't you go home for visits?"

"Home? Naw. Not since my parents moved. Richmond isn't home for me. But I see them periodically. Depends where I am at the time. Last year they went to Hawaii over Christmas with my sister and her husband. I celebrated with this very nice retired couple in an RV campground. The wife bought one of those complete turkey dinners from a grocery store and heated it up in their oven."

"Sounds terrible."

"It wasn't." He flashed a melancholy grin. "They had a lot of interesting stories."

"But you do see them, right? Your parents and your sister?"

"Sure. And we talk regularly. Especially on holidays. Well, except for Valentine's Day."

"Right." Ronnie swallowed. The painful lump that had formed moments ago remained stubbornly lodged.

"I'm not fit company on that day, and I don't even try to be. The folks and sis have learned to leave me alone."

"How did they take it? When you and I broke…" *Oh, just say it*, she told herself. "When I left?"

"They felt bad, of course. They were fond of you."

"Same here. They're great."

"We're not as close as we should be." Nate propped his back against the pasture gate. "My fault. They only wanted to help, but I preferred to remain miserable and would have none of their… I believe *interference* was the term I used. And I was angry at Mom for a long time because of what she said to you."

This seemed like a good spot to ease into what Ronnie predicted would be the difficult part of their discussion.

"That, too, is my fault."

"Don't beat yourself up over it. We're okay now. Not back to where we were before but better."

She glanced away, the sadness in Nate's expression too great for her to bear. They'd only just shared the good news with their families a month earlier. Nate had been on the phone with his mom the day before. His next calls had been to relay unfortunate news.

"When I thought about all the people who were affected by my actions," she said, "not just you and me but our parents and sisters, too, I dreaded facing them again."

"Why? Everyone was sympathetic."

Speaking had become difficult. Ronnie mustered her courage before continuing. "I was convinced they'd think me a horrible person."

"You didn't cause the miscarriage."

"I insisted on competing at Nationals. You didn't want me to. My dad and sisters told me not to go. And if I'd stayed home instead, I wouldn't have tripped and fallen."

She shut her eyes and saw again the riderless horse

charging toward her. Felt her body seize with fear as her legs struggled in vain to carry her to safety, only to have her feet tangle beneath her. Experienced the hard, heavy hit when the ground rushed up to meet her. Heard the chorus of alarmed voices, Nate's the loudest.

At first, she'd been simply stunned. An hour later, after the rodeo medic had examined her and insisted she rest, she'd believed herself to be fine. Two hours later, the cramping and bleeding had started and her worst nightmare had come true shortly after she and Nate reached the hospital.

"You didn't fall when you competed," Nate said. "And that's what we argued about. I still wanted you to come and watch me. You might have wound up in the path of that horse no matter what."

"I doubt it. If I hadn't competed, I would have been sitting in the bleachers, not standing where I was."

"We can play the what-if game all night and get nowhere."

"You were so mad at me." She crossed her arms, as much to fend off the encroaching cold as to shore up her defenses. "You wanted the baby, and I saw how much losing it affected you."

"It was an accident, Ronnie. An awful, unavoidable accident. The doctor even said the fall wasn't that bad. He wondered about the health of the fetus and said you may have miscarried anyway at some point."

Nonviable pregnancy. Those were the words the doctor had used. They hadn't lessened any of Ronnie's anguish. Or guilt.

"We'll never know, will we?" And that was what tormented her. Steeling her resolve, she continued. "I was unfair to you. You had a right. A say. The decision whether I competed or not wasn't solely mine to make. I was selfish, and we all paid the price."

Her dream since her very first rodeo had been to win a World title. Nate's, too, but he'd had a dozen titles to his name and thought nothing of missing a year. He hadn't understood her reluctance to take time off. Her agony of going to Vegas five years in a row and losing all five times. She'd begun doubting she had the talent and determination to succeed.

Tears stung her eyes, and she wiped them away. "I wasn't entirely reckless, Nate. I talked to my doctor beforehand. He said riding was a personal choice. That I was experienced and as long as I didn't fall, the baby would be fine. I also talked to some friends on the circuit. Mary Simmons, you remember her? She competed up until her twelfth week with no problems. I never expected to be nearly run down by a horse, but I should have been more careful."

Ronnie had lain awake for hours in her hospital bed while Nate dozed in the chair beside her—when he wasn't consoling her or shedding tears with her. He'd also phoned her father and his parents, who'd arrived the next morning, and conferred with the doctors regarding her care. All in all, he'd been the best, most loving, most supportive partner she could have asked for.

And how had she rewarded him? By rejecting his beautiful, heartfelt Valentine's Day proposal and walking out two days later while he was helping a buddy teach steer wrestling to a group of 4-H members.

"I don't blame you," Nate said.

Yeah, well, how come he kept his distance, not inching closer to her as he'd done at every opportunity since his return?

"I had a lot of dark emotions in the weeks following the miscarriage."

"Trust me, if there's one thing I'm familiar with, it's dark emotions."

She nodded. "I started examining my whole life. My drive for a title and the reasons behind it. My skewed priorities. Where we were in our relationship. I looked deep inside myself, tried to figure out why I'd put winning ahead of me and you and our baby."

"I don't believe you caused the miscarriage," he repeated. "It just happened."

"The more I thought about things, the more convinced I became your mom was right about what she said to me, and the more immersed in guilt I became."

"I wasn't blind, Ronnie. I realized you were having problems coping."

"Yes." She sniffed. "You were wonderful. Gave me space when I needed it. Held me when I cried."

"I must have let you down somehow, some way."

"The more you tried to help, the worse I felt. Then, you took me out to that beautiful restaurant for an incredible dinner and proposed." She wiped her damp cheek. "I got scared."

Confusion flashed in his eyes. "Of what?"

"I wasn't sure why you proposed."

"Why does anyone propose? I loved you."

"Believe me, I came up with a lot of reasons. Does he truly want to spend the rest of his life with me? Is he asking out of duty and a sense of responsibility? Is he just trying to help me through my grief and make me feel better? Has he noticed me pulling away and is afraid of losing me? Is he trying to prove to both of us he doesn't hate me for what I did?"

"I never have and never will hate you, Ronnie."

"But you resented me."

"Not true, I swear." He rubbed his forehead in obvious frustration. "Not for that."

She resisted saying, "See! Told you," and instead asked, "What, then? For leaving?"

"Leaving without a word. Refusing to return my phone calls. Making me feel like what happened was my fault."

"I'm sorry, Nate. I realized I was being awful. You deserved much, much better. But I was worried you'd track me down and convince me to come back with you."

"I might have."

"To what end? Seriously. A quick, clean break was better."

"I loved you. We were good together," he insisted.

"I thought so, too. And, then, all at once, we weren't good together. We faced our first big challenges and look what happened. I shut down emotionally and you overcompensated. We were caught in a vicious circle with only one escape. I took it."

"You didn't give us enough time to heal." The anger she'd been expecting finally erupted. His terse voice sliced through her with the pain of a razor sharp blade. "Instead, you abandoned me. Us. Our life and entire future."

"You're right." She didn't offer yet another apology. "And now you know why I didn't want you staying here."

"Me leaving would make things easier on you."

"On you, too."

"Running away might be your style, but it's not mine."

That was harsh. Possibly deserved but harsh nonetheless.

He pushed off the gate. "I've finally found something, two things, that give me a reason to get up in the morning. Theo McGraw and recreational bull riding."

"I am happy for you."

"Except you'd be happier if I rediscovered my purpose somewhere other than Mustang Valley."

He walked away then, not letting her finish everything she'd intended to say. A taste of her own medicine, she supposed.

"I assume we're in agreement," she said to his retreating back. "We keep our relationship strictly professional."

"For now," he called over his shoulder.

"OF COURSE YOU'RE GOING." Mel adjusted her very pregnant body in the thick cushioned recliner while attempting to glare at Ronnie. Her floundering lessened the effect considerably. "Even if I have to drag you there."

She was referring to the opening night bull riding event at the Poco Dinero. Before Nate's arrival a week-and-a-half ago, Ronnie wouldn't have missed attending for anything. Now, doubts plagued her, especially since their talk the past Sunday.

They hadn't parted on the best of terms. He'd come to Sam's practice on Wednesday but had sat with Theo rather than Ronnie. He'd also avoided her at work. Or she'd avoided him; hard to tell which. A minor miracle considering the many hours they were spending in preparation of their respective events.

Just this morning, the bulls from the Lost Dutchman Livestock Company had arrived. Ronnie had happened to drive by the bar on her way to the post office and spotted the large silver trailer parked alongside the arena. There had also been a half dozen cowboys on the scene busily working. She hadn't recognized Nate among them, not that she'd been looking.

Okay, okay. She *had* looked. Briefly.

"There's no reason I need to be there until tomorrow

morning," Ronnie told Mel. "Late entry sign-ups don't start until noon."

"You can't miss the first night," Mel insisted. "We're all going. Dad and Dolores. Frankie, Spence and the twins. Aaron's even bringing Kaylee."

At the mention of Ronnie's stepniece, her resolve softened. It would be fun seeing the excitement on the youngster's face. She hadn't grown up in a horse town like the rest of Ronnie's family, who'd all seen countless rodeos.

"I don't know." Ronnie's resolve wavered in spite of her determination to remain firm.

"It's Nate, right?" Her always astute sister naturally pinpointed the problem. "You're avoiding him."

"Yes."

There was no point in lying. Mel would see straight through her.

They sat in the living room of the house they'd once shared. Mel had moved out this past summer when she and Aaron had fallen in love and decided to marry. Naturally, Ronnie was glad for her sister and absolutely adored Aaron and his daughter, Kaylee. The downside was, having to pay the entire rent and utilities on her own significantly strained her monthly budget.

She hated the thought of dipping into the remaining money earmarked for her business, the money her father had gifted her from his lottery winnings. Besides, not much was left.

Which was why recruiting new clients and students had become crucial. Mel made a valid point when she asked what better place to meet potential clients and students than at a rodeo event a large number of horse enthusiasts were likely to attend? Ronnie would be a fool not to take advantage.

"We've reached an agreement of sorts. Strictly business. Nothing personal."

Mel pushed awkwardly up from her chair, stomach first. "Are things that bad between you? I noticed you didn't talk much at the cookout."

"I avoided him."

"Was that really necessary?"

"Probably not. Which is why I went to see him at The Small Change afterward. We had a—" Ronnie searched for the right words "—terse exchange. Some things were said."

"Do tell." Mel reached behind her and rubbed the small of her back as if to soothe an ache lodged there.

"I felt I owed him an explanation for why I suddenly left and didn't return his calls."

"Finally! After six years. That was mighty considerate of you."

Ronnie ignored her sister's sarcastic tone. "It's not like he had no clue."

"What you did to him wasn't nice."

Apparently the gloves were off. Both Ronnie's sisters had been solicitous and compassionate when she'd first come home, respecting her wish not to discuss the painful details of her and Nate's breakup. She should have realized they'd side with him.

Well, who wouldn't? He'd done nothing wrong, after all. She hadn't wanted to admit it back then, which was why she'd refused to talk to him or answer his calls. Selfish, yes. Cruel, probably. She knew she owed him an apology.

Neither of her sisters had made a secret of their continued fondness for him since his unexpected appearance. Frankie had recently referred to Nate as the prize

Ronnie let get away. More salt in an old wound, and it had burned.

"Rest assured—" Ronnie also pushed to her feet "—I took a verbal beating from Nate for my inconsiderate behavior."

"He has a right to be angry. He stood by you, didn't blame you for the miscarriage and defended you to his mom even when it damaged his relationship with his entire family. And don't forget he proposed. Most women would do anything for a boyfriend like that."

"I made a decision at the time that I thought was the right one. We were miserable, and I saw no sense prolonging the inevitable."

"Be honest, *you* were miserable. Him, not as much and only because of how you treated him."

The remark hit home, as Mel had surely intended. Ronnie swallowed and attempted to shake off the pain.

"All right, *I* was miserable. Drowning in it and seeing no end. I truly thought that by cutting all ties and getting away quickly, Nate and I could move on and heal."

That was what her father had done with Sam's mother at the end of their affair. Granted, the circumstances were entirely different, and Ronnie hadn't known about the affair at the time of her breakup with Nate. But upon learning about it, she'd empathized with her father.

On that one aspect, anyway. Other aspects, like her father's lying, had required more time to get past.

"Only you didn't move on and heal," Mel said. "Neither you nor Nate."

Had she and Frankie learned about Nate's difficulties these past years? Ronnie didn't ask, insisting, "We're fine. Just peachy."

"You were selfish." Mel apparently wasn't done scolding Ronnie. "Thinking only of yourself."

"Not true! I couldn't marry him, and staying would have just given him false hope."

Mel sent her an accusing look. "Neither of you has been in a serious relationship since your split. He practically dropped off the face of the earth while you ran home and went into hiding."

"I'm not hiding!"

"Oh, please." Mel rolled her eyes and sat back down on the recliner, sinking all the way up to her elbows. "When's the last time you went on a date? Or anywhere that didn't involve a student and a rodeo or a family gathering?"

"I'm helping the mustang sanctuary with their booth at the Holly Daze Festival next week."

Mel uttered a sound of disgust. "That doesn't count."

"I'm too busy to date."

"Maybe what you are is still in love with Nate and he with you."

"You couldn't be more wrong." She spoke forcefully, as much to convince herself as Mel.

"Attending the bull riding event tonight will go a long way in showing Nate there are no hard feelings and you support him."

Ronnie grumbled under her breath.

"Come on. Half the town will be there and surely people from Scottsdale and Cave Creek and maybe even farther away. Bring a big stack of business cards to pass out."

"You've convinced me." Ronnie threw up her hands in surrender. "But only because I want to show you how wrong you are. Plus, I do need to recruit a few more barrel racers for tomorrow if I hope to make a decent showing."

"We'll swing by at six to pick you up."

"Thanks, but I'll drive myself."

"Oh? Planning an early escape and need your own set of wheels?"

"Will you quit it? I'm not planning an escape." She heaved a frustrated groan. "You win. Be here at six."

Mel laughed and was still laughing when she waddled out the front door a short time later. Her leaving couldn't have come soon enough for Ronnie, who'd been getting ready to give her sister the boot regardless of her out-to-there pregnant belly.

She took her time getting dressed for the evening. Best jeans. Shiny red leather boots. The robin's-egg blue western-cut shirt with red piping. Her favorite Kate Spade purse that she'd scrimped and saved for half a year to buy. A touch more makeup than usual, only because floodlights tended to give her face a washed-out appearance and *not* to impress Nate.

Rather than accompanying her family to the arena, she had them drop her off in front of the Poco Dinero. She wanted to chat briefly with Bess's assistant manager and check on the status of sign-ups for tomorrow.

The very first thing she noticed was new posters on the walls alongside the ones advertising the recreational rodeo events. These were for the annual Valentine's Day dance and dinner, less than three months away.

Bess had been hosting the event for the past ten or twelve years and always gave it a big push. Ronnie had attended with her sisters back before she'd met Nate, and once with him when they'd stopped for a short visit on their way to a rodeo.

How could she have forgotten about the dance and dinner? Especially since Frankie had mentioned repeatedly at Sam's celebration cookout that she'd be catering the dinner. But Ronnie had forgotten, or at least put it from her mind. Seeing the posters triggered a shock wave that left her momentarily disconcerted.

Nate wasn't the only one not fit for company during the traditionally romantic holiday. Ronnie also preferred keeping to herself on Valentine's Day, memories of Nate's romantic proposal and her gut-wrenching rejection assailing her.

All right, dammit. Mel was right. Again. Ronnie had retreated to the security and solitude of her home and family after leaving Nate. She hadn't dated at all her first year home and only occasionally since then. Less chance of being hurt again.

She'd refused to acknowledge the depths of her grief after losing the baby, made worse by the insensitive remarks Nate's mother had made at the hospital when Ronnie was at her most vulnerable. Add to that her refusal to talk about what had happened with anyone, including Nate, and it had been easy to build an emotional wall around herself.

Just like Nate had. The only difference between them was he'd taken his voluntary seclusion on the road.

It was no way for either of them to live, and they were both paying a steep price. Ronnie had lost, no, given up, a man she'd loved to distraction. She'd also lost her life-long dream of having a family, something she'd planned on starting right after winning a World Championship. On one fateful day, her entire future had been altered.

Not altered, Ronnie reminded herself. Her dream of a family absolutely remained within reach. But every version of that dream included Nate. She'd been the one to let fear of loss, grief, guilt, and the imagined accusation she saw in his eyes drive a wedge between them.

How to break the cycle? She wanted to, just couldn't

seem to accomplish it. Okay, that was wrong, too. She was simply too scared. Hiding out was easier.

Her glance landed once again on the Valentine's Day posters. There'd be no rodeo events that night, or probably not. Bess hadn't said either way yet. What if Ronnie went to the dance—with a date? That would show Nate and her sisters and everyone else she was over him. Had moved on and healed.

If he was still in Mustang Valley come February. Both of his jobs were on a trial basis, and things might not work out. Very likely, he'd get the itch to hop in his truck and travel to a new destination, as had been his habit these past six years.

What did it matter? She'd go on a date regardless, even if she had to ask the guy herself. Enrico's nephew had recently started working at The Small Change. He was attractive and, like her, in his late twenties. He'd also been more than a little friendly to her the last couple of times they'd run into each other.

Decision made, Ronnie headed to the office to locate Elena, the assistant manager. To her relief, Elena reported that three more participants had signed up for the barrel racing. Ronnie wouldn't be humiliated by low entries for her first event.

Next, she strolled through the packed bar area and out the rear service door to the arena. Her family was already there and hailed her from their seats in the bleachers. If not for their waves and shouts, she wouldn't have spotted them. The stands were filled to their 150-person capacity.

While climbing the steps, she noticed Theo McGraw sitting with her family. Not entirely unexpected—her father did work for the man and often gave him lifts around town.

It was also possible Nate had brought Theo. Not only

had the older man accompanied Nate to one of Sam's practices, he'd been spotted riding as a passenger in Nate's truck often enough people were commenting.

Many of the remarks were about Theo looking healthier than he had for some time and getting around better. Also that his mood was considerably improved. All in a week and a half? Apparently Nate was the miracle worker Reese had called him, which, Ronnie supposed, decreased the chances of his part-time caregiver job not working out.

For nearly six years he'd been traveling the country in search of a new direction and the emotional respite he so desperately needed.

Was it a coincidence he was finding both in the town Ronnie called home? She was beginning to think maybe not.

Chapter Eight

"There you are," Ronnie's father said when she finally reached her family's row in the stands.

Everyone automatically shifted over to make room for her, everyone being her dad, stepmom, Frankie, Spence, their twin daughters, Mel, Aaron and his daughter, who happened to be best buddies with the twins.

Quite the gathering, Ronnie observed. The Hartman clan was growing and would grow again with the birth of Mel's baby. Ronnie was the only sister currently unattached. Even Sam had a boyfriend—the geeky tech student who worshipped the ground she walked on.

Ronnie insisted she didn't care. She was fine with her single status, thank you very much.

"Isn't this exciting?" Frankie nudged her in the side.

She'd squeezed in next to her oldest sister after waving and saying hello to the rest of her family.

Theo occupied a seat in the middle and, if Ronnie wasn't mistaken, was flirting a bit with the middle-aged woman in front of him. Honestly, did he never quit trying? Fortunately, the woman appeared to consider his overtures harmless and played along.

"Fingers crossed nobody gets hurt the first night," Frankie commented. "Bess is taking a real chance. A bad reputation could ruin her business."

Ronnie didn't agree. "Wild Bill's did really well with their recreational bull riding, and they had a few injuries over the years. It's unavoidable and part of the appeal. You don't know these cowboys like I do. They love the adrenaline rush and the thrill of walking away un-scathed."

The restaurant in north Scottsdale had indeed been a popular spot for recreational bull riders. That was until their main building had burned to the ground, the result of an electrical fire.

"I do too know cowboys," Frankie countered. "I'm getting married to one."

"When is that, by the way?"

"We're thinking of March. We didn't want to steal any of Mel and Aaron's thunder. Let them enjoy being the newlyweds in the family for a while."

Ronnie listened to her sister while scanning the arena and holding pens for Nate. Several wranglers were herd-ing the first of the bulls along the narrow, enclosed aisle connecting the pens and the bucking chutes. Excitement among the spectators noticeably mounted.

Just like at any regular, sanctioned rodeo, cowboys sat atop the fences, hung from the rails or straddled the buck-ing chute walls. A good many men wore protective vests and helmets, a practice Ronnie heartily endorsed. When Nate had competed, he'd claimed the helmet blocked his vision and threw off his balance. It had been their one big, unresolved argument.

If she brought up the subject today, he'd remind her that his worst injury had occurred when he'd fallen from the green-broke horse, miles away from the nearest bull. He'd say, "Just goes to show you there are no guarantees."

Every competitor tonight had signed a waiver and release of liability form. If not, they would be banned from the arena. The barrel racers were required to sign the same waiver and release. No one had raised a single eyebrow at this standard practice.

Also like any regulation rodeo, two bullfighters

roamed the arena and interacted with the crowd, particularly the children. Easily identified by their painted faces, straw cowboy hats and oversize denim cutoffs, their first job was to protect the cowboy from charging bulls, and their second was to entertain. They often took bigger risks than the men riding the bulls, and Ronnie greatly admired their courage.

Hearing a rapid-fire trio of ear-splitting clangs, she looked over at the chutes to see a large black bull raising a ruckus. Kicking first with his hind legs, he rose up and thrust all of his eighteen hundred pounds forward. If not confined by the small space and high walls, he would have jumped out and likely charged the nearest person.

On closer inspection, the nearest person was Nate! He clung to the chute wall, half in and half out.

Ronnie instantly rose from her seat only to sit back down when Nate hauled himself to safety. The bull's horns had missed him by perhaps two inches, but they had missed him.

The next moment, he was hollering orders to the nearby hired wranglers. He then turned to the young man beside him, the first competitor to go according to the number he wore on his back. He was also the one about to ride this mammoth, uncontrolled beast. Judging by his expression, he was reconsidering.

Nate patted the man on the back before heading off. The next minute, Ronnie lost sight of him. She tried not to let her anxiety show and buried her balled fists in the pockets of her hoodie.

"Nervous or excited?" Frankie asked.

"Both. I really hope tonight is a success."

"Are you kidding? The place is packed. Bess is making money hand over fist."

Ronnie hoped so, for Nate as well as herself.

"You should be down there mingling and pitching your school, not sitting up here."

"I will. Later."

"Do you recognize any of the competitors?"

"Some," Ronnie said. "I've seen them at different rodeos. But I don't watch bull riding like I used to."

"Nate probably knows them all."

"Maybe." Ronnie squinted her eyes against the bright glare of the floodlights. "Isn't that Enrico's nephew in the blue shirt and white cowboy hat? Is he competing?"

"I'd say yes. He's wearing a vest."

"I had no idea he rode bulls."

"He must have some experience or he wouldn't have signed up."

"Yeah. Maybe. Or he's completely lacking common sense." Perhaps she should reconsider asking him to be her date for the Valentine's Day dance and dinner.

Frankie drew back and scrutinized Ronnie. "Are you interested in him?"

"I've met him at the ranch. He seems nice, and he's Enrico's nephew. I wouldn't want him to get hurt if only for that reason. He just started working at The Small Change. I'm surprised Enrico is letting him compete."

"I gave anyone who wanted to participate the day off with pay," Theo interjected. He sat on the other side of Spence and had obviously overheard Ronnie and Frankie talking. "My way of supporting Bess."

"That was generous of you," Frankie said.

"I try to do my part for the community."

No one could ever say differently. The Small Change Ranch was currently home to the mustang sanctuary where over two hundred formerly neglected and homeless mustangs resided. The ranch had also hosted the last several adoption auctions, raising money and awareness for the plight of wild horses. During the last auction, Theo had paid for the construction of a mile-long track where three mustangs had run in a mock race, resulting in the largest fund-raiser to date.

"How are things working out with Nate?" Frankie asked Theo while sending Ronnie a mischievous wink.

"He annoys the hell out of me, if you must know." A smile pulled at his mouth and mirth shone in his eyes. "I rue the day my daughter hired him."

"That good?" Frankie nudged Ronnie again. "Glad to hear it."

"I suppose as far as nurses go he's not the worst I've had."

Nate wasn't a nurse, or even an accredited caregiver, as he'd made clear to Reese when she'd offered him the job. Theo had probably used the first word that came to mind.

The PA system abruptly crackled and Bess's voice came on, alerting everyone to the start of the event. Following that, she made a series of announcements about safety requirements, the schedule, the rules and the all-important prizes.

"First, second and third place will do all right," Frankie commented. "There's a fair amount of money up for grabs."

Ronnie pointed to a group of competitors clustered by the fence. "Look, there's a woman suited up to ride."

"Where?" Frankie gasped. "You're right."

Before Ronnie could say more, a huge commotion erupted at the bucking chutes. Shouting warnings to get back, cowboys threw themselves off the chutes to the ground, only to scramble backward. A few daring souls reached their arms into the chute, mindless of the wildly thrashing bull, the same black beast who'd made such a fuss earlier.

Suddenly, the bull humped up, his huge, muscular back appearing above the high walls.

"My God," someone hollered. "There's a man trapped in there with him."

Ronnie leaned forward in her seat for a better view, along with the entire stand of spectators.

"It's Nate," her father said, his voice filled with alarm.

She didn't wait to hear the rest. In a flash, she was on her feet and running down the steps. At the bottom, she turned toward the bucking chutes, silently praying that Nate wasn't hurt. Or worse.

NATE FIGURED HE'D seen bulls from just about every angle possible. Flat on his back. Flying through the air. Leaning so far forward over their necks he'd nose-planted between their horns. Bent so far backward his head banged against their spring-loaded rumps. Through the rails of a fence or the slats of a pen or the opening in a trailer. Plenty of those views had been with him dusting off his jeans and watching as the bull was herded out of the arena.

Not once, though, had he gotten a closeup of the animal's massive body from three inches away, his entire lower half pinned between the bull's flank and the metal wall of a bucking chute.

One second longer and he'd have been crushed like an aluminum can, his life flashing before his eyes. He didn't enjoy admitting that even after being pulled from harm's way by four pairs of strong hands, his heart still beat with the force of a jackhammer and sweat coated every inch of his skin.

"That was mighty close," Spence Bohanan said, relief in his voice.

"Yeah, a little too close." Nate managed a weak grin for Frankie's fiancé.

After sharing a beer at the Poco Dinero two evenings earlier, Spence had agreed to lend Nate a hand with the bull riding events. Considering Spence was one of the men who'd pulled Nate to safety, he was damn glad he'd asked.

It felt good making a friend in town. More than one if he counted Theo.

"I owe you big-time," Nate said to Spence. "You could have been hurt saving me."

"Nothing you wouldn't do for me in return."

It was true, and not just because of an unspoken cowboy code. Nate genuinely liked Spence.

"Let me by, let me by! Nate, my God, are you all right? Answer me."

Nate turned to see Ronnie pushing through the small crowd surrounding him as if digging herself out of quicksand. She wore the same concerned expression she had countless times in the past when she'd rushed over after he'd been thrown from a bull or narrowly avoided the kick of an angry steer.

"If I were any better, I'd be ten feet tall."

Funny, he hadn't uttered that expression in years. If fact, he'd forgotten about it until now.

She reached him and, after a moment's hesitation, threw herself into his arms. Clinging tight, she said, "Stop joking."

"I'm fine. Feel around while you're at it. No broken bones."

He thought she might pull away at his reference to her hanging-on-for-dear-life hug. Instead, she gripped him even tighter. His pulse skyrocketed, this time for an entirely different reason. He quite enjoyed having her anchored to him, their bodies connecting in all the right places. In another minute, he'd stop caring where they were and who was watching and kiss her. He just might do it anyway.

"You scared me," she said, her warm breath skimming across the patch of exposed skin above his shirt collar.

Forgetting about Spence and the bull and the crowd in the bleachers, he centered his attention on Ronnie. "Scared myself, too."

They'd agreed after last Sunday that any involvement was a bad idea. Holding her and reacquainting himself with the lovely curves hidden beneath her hoodie, Nate couldn't help reconsidering.

"What happened?" She attempted to ease away from him.

He didn't let go, refusing to end the moment. But reality returned, and the curious stares searing into them had him dropping his arm. Reluctantly. While he didn't care who saw them, Ronnie might.

"Damn strap came loose and slipped down. I thought I could grab it quick. Mad Max wasn't too keen on sharing his personal space. Rather than politely ask me to leave, he tried to flatten me."

"You could have been killed."

"Not likely."

He played down the incident rather than giving her more reason to worry. Nate's descent into the chute had actually sent the bull into a rage. It was a minor miracle he'd escaped unscathed.

Then again, if he embellished the story, there was a chance Ronnie would fly into his arms again.

Spence came over, thwarting Nate's plan. "He's one lucky guy."

"Me or the bull?" Nate chuckled, though it sounded a bit thin to his ears.

"Stop doing that." Ronnie sighed with exasperation. "You don't have to put yourself in danger anymore. You quit rodeoing, remember?"

"Believe me, cozying up with Mad Max wasn't in my plans. It just happened."

"Come on, Truett," urged the cowboy who'd drawn the number one spot. "Let's get this show on the road."

"Be right there." If the man was raring to ride Mad Max after witnessing what had happened, who was Nate to stop him? "Gimme a second." To Ronnie he said, "I have to go."

"Okay. But be careful." She laid a hand on his chest. "Promise me."

"You should be saying that to these guys, not me."

"I mean it, Nate."

Oh, what the hell? Wrapping an arm around her waist, he brought his mouth close to hers. "Here I thought you were immune to my charms."

"I am." She reached up and cradled his cheeks before brushing her lips across his.

The effect was immediate as emotions he'd kept buried for so long pushed to the surface. He tamped them down with the last of his willpower.

"You always were a terrible liar, sweetheart." If they weren't surrounded, he'd show her just how crazy she was making him. "Wait for me when this is over."

Suddenly coy, she answered, "I may be here. I may not."

"Wherever you are, I'll find you. Count on it."

She left then, at a considerably slower pace than when she'd arrived. Nate should have been gearing up for the start of the bull riding. Instead, he stood there unable to move until Ronnie was swallowed by the crowd.

Spence returned to stand beside him. "You two back together?"

"Nope."

"Could've fooled me."

"Old habits."

"Yeah, I hear you. Did I tell you yet about me and Frankie and when I came back to town? She was an old habit *I* couldn't break. Women are funny that way."

Slowly, reason returned to Nate's mashed-potato brain. As much as he wanted to hunt Ronnie down later and pick up where they'd left off, a better course of action would be continuing their discussion from the other day. Not a single piece of the baggage the two of them carried had been unpacked and put away. Getting involved before that occurred was unwise if not downright stupid.

Nate made his way to the bucking chutes where he oversaw the night's competition. The thirty-one brave souls were quickly trimmed down to eleven after the first round, then down to six for the final round. Two hours of rip-roaring fun and edge-of-the-seat excitement concluded with the top three competitors receiving their respective shares of the pot and a round of wild applause from the audience.

At the end of the event, Bess's voice blared from the speakers, inviting everyone to return the next afternoon for the barrel racing at two and bull riding at seven sharp. She also announced well drinks and draft beer were half price until ten.

Many people stayed, and the celebrating continued inside the Poco Dinero, as was Bess's intention. Nate helped the hands from the Lost Dutchman Livestock Company settle the bulls for the night in the holding pens, giving them fresh feed and water.

Eventually, after what felt like an eternity, Nate was done for the evening. The facility was back in order, the arena graded for tomorrow, equipment stowed and padlocks double-checked. Bess brought out free longnecks for Nate and his crew. They didn't refuse, not after the hard night's work.

"Thank you, ma'am," Nate said, accepting the beer she held out to him and indulging in a healthy swig. He then wiped his damp forehead with the back of his other hand. "That hits the spot."

"Thought you'd like to know." She took his arm and pulled him aside. "We did okay tonight. Took in enough entry fees to cover the livestock rental and the prize money."

"That's good."

She gave a rusty cackle. "Good enough for a first night. I'm hoping to do better next weekend."

Nate wasn't sure what to make of that remark. How many entry fees were needed to turn a profit? "Should I change strategies?"

"You just keep doing what you're doing." She patted him fondly on the arm. "The money will come."

He almost asked her if Ronnie was inside or if she'd left, but changed his mind. Spence and several of the other guys were already ribbing him. He didn't need his boss concerned about the potentially negative consequences of her employees fraternizing.

"Has Theo left yet?" Nate asked instead.

"Enrico took him home. Did you see his nephew? Well, of course you did. Heck of a bull rider."

"Who'd have guessed he only competed a couple times in high school?"

"Not me. He said you have the night off, by the way. Theo, not Enrico's nephew."

That explained the cryptic text Nate had received earlier from Reese. "Good. Not that I'm complaining, but it's been a long day."

"Go on inside. Have yourself a little fun before you head home. You've earned it."

"That's an offer hard to refuse."

They went in together. Once through the door, Bess headed to the bar while Nate went in search of Ronnie. He found her, along with her dad and stepmom, just as they were putting on their coats and getting ready to leave.

"Taking off already?" He flashed his winningest grin.

"Us old folks retire early," Dolores answered and linked arms with her husband. "Even on a Friday night."

"Heck of show." Ray shook Nate's hand. "Good job, son."

"Are you coming back tomorrow?"

"In the afternoon. For the barrel racing. You going to be here?"

Nate had told Ronnie he'd stay away rather than cause her any discomfort. That was before she'd come flying down from the stands and they'd shared a brief, electrifying kiss.

Catching her glance, he attempted to read her expression. She didn't appear uncomfortable or dismayed by her dad's question.

"I might." He lifted a shoulder in an unconcerned shrug. "Probably."

Ronnie further surprised him by saying, "Come. I could use you in the cheering section. I'm worried no one will show."

"Won't happen. People will be here in droves." He resisted reaching out to reassure her. "By the way, drum up any new business tonight?"

"One contact. An acquaintance of the Carringtons."

"She a barrel racer?"

"No, a recreational rider. Purchased one of the mustangs at the last adoption event and apparently he spooks easily. She wants someone with experience to train him."

"You're expanding your business. Congratulations."

"I'm not sure I'm qualified. Recreational riding is different from barrel racing."

"You'll do great."

"We'll see." Ronnie zipped up her hoodie. "See you tomorrow."

"Stay," Dolores told Ronnie, a glint of mischief in her eyes. "You can talk horses."

"You're my ride home."

The glint in Dolores's eyes brightened. "I'm sure Nate will drive you."

"Happy to," he agreed, deciding he liked Ronnie's new stepmom.

Ronnie gnawed on her lower lip. "I'm not sure..."

"Come on, honey." Dolores nudged Ray. "It's late, and I'm tired."

Ronnie could have gone after her dad and stepmom, but she didn't, leaving Nate to wonder...and hope.

"Since we're here and the music's playing," he said, "would you like to dance?"

She shook her head. "That'll only get us in trouble."

He grinned. "Trouble can be fun."

"Trouble can also be trouble. And besides, I see a couple of people I need to talk to."

He let her go, confident she'd soon be sitting beside

him in his truck. Considering that the last time they'd ridden together they'd kissed, she was no safer with him there than the Poco Dinero dance floor.

Chapter Nine

"You don't have to walk me to the door."

"Too late." Nate climbed out of his truck and met her on the passenger side.

He wasn't ready for the night to end. Could be he was keyed up from the bull riding event and his close call with Mad Max in the bucking chute. Having Ronnie sitting next to him the entire drive home, reliving the sensation of her locked in his arms and the sweet taste of her lips, was a more likely reason.

"Nice digs," he commented, pulling into the driveway. She pressed the button on her key ring that remotely opened the garage door and activated an overhead light.

"How long have you been a member of the homeowner's club?"

"Actually, I'm just renting. Though, I can see myself owning a house like this one day."

"You live alone?"

She shot him a perturbed look.

"Hey, I was curious. Rent can't be cheap."

"Mel was living with me until recently. Which is why I agreed to help Bess with the barrel racing. I find myself in need of a second revenue stream."

They went into the garage, passing stacks of storage boxes, Christmas decorations, a worktable, an old bicycle and the usual assortment of items stored in a garage.

"Looking for a new roommate?" he asked.

That earned him another look, this one annoyed.

"I wasn't volunteering." He had, however, been trying to get a rise out of her just for fun.

At the door, she inserted her key. "Thanks for the lift, Nate."

When she turned to face him, he pulled her into a snug embrace. "Now, where were we?"

She rested her hands on his shoulders, not quite pushing him away but sending a message. "This isn't a good idea."

"No? I've had worse ones."

"We agreed to avoid this exact thing."

He walked her back a step until she was wedged between him and the door. Already, he could feel his body responding.

"That was before you came racing down from the stands and bowled over a dozen innocent people to see if I was hurt."

"I didn't bowl anyone over. Granted, I hurried."

"Tell that to those innocent people nursing bruises."

"You're incorrigible."

He grinned. "But am I impossible to resist?"

"Fine." She huffed. "One kiss." Before he could devour her, she withdrew and narrowed her gaze at him. "A chaste one."

Like hell. He had Ronnie in his arms, right where he wanted her. For a moment, just one, he intended to forget about all the obstacles they faced and the ones in the past responsible for ending their relationship. He wanted to be the people they once were, young and head over heels in love.

"Sorry." Removing his cowboy hat, he set it on top of a nearby storage cabinet. "No can do."

Her eyes widened. "Nate."

He also removed her cowboy hat and placed it next

his. "Be warned, sweetheart. This is going to be good. I hope you're ready."

"Wait."

Groaning with frustration, he said, "First, I can't get you to talk to me. Now, I can't get you to stop."

"We need to be clear on a few things first. Just because I'm letting you kiss me doesn't mean we're—"

He was through listening and silenced her the best way he knew how. Planting his mouth firmly on hers, he took advantage of her parted lips. She resisted again, sending his frustration through the roof. Did she need to initiate every kiss in order to be a willing participant?

Increasing the pressure, he coaxed rather than demanded a response from her. Encouraged instead of insisted. Finally, she ceased resisting and arched into him.

This, he thought with pleasure, *is more like it.* Her ardor rose to match his—hot and hungry, the way he remembered. The way he'd been dreaming of every day since his return. Desire so intense it invaded his every cell. Need so demanding it consumed him.

When they finally broke apart, he was the one weak in the knees and out of breath. Holding on and waiting for his strength to return, he murmured her name against her cheek.

Like him, she needed a moment to recover. When she finally spoke, her voice was unsteady. "That was, ah…"

She was at a loss, unable to continue, which was how he most liked seeing her. Vulnerable. With her guard down and her heart laid bare. This was the Ronnie who could be easily hurt. It was also the Ronnie he could reach. Affect. Ronnie at her most honest.

"It was fantastic," he said.

A tiny smile tugged at her lips. "We did get some things right, you and I."

Yeah, and kissing was one of them. "Invite me inside."

"Whoa there, cowboy." Her guard instantly shot up.

"What are those ground rules you mentioned earlier? Let's review them."

She straightened and squeezed her eyes shut. "You're impossible."

"Invite me in, Ronnie. We can talk or not talk. It's entirely up to you. I don't want to go back to my cold, cramped trailer. I want to sit with you on a couch with my feet up and my arm around you. Notice I said sit on a couch and not lie in a bed."

She stared at the floor for a long moment before lifting her gaze to his. "I'm probably going to regret this."

"Yes!" He grabbed her hand, pushed open the door and pulled her inside the house before she had a chance to change her mind.

From the laundry room they entered a short hall that opened into a kitchen. While half the size of the Mc-Graws', the room was cozy and the decor inviting.

Nate had no interest. He wasn't here to cook.

"Where's the living room?" he asked, stripping off his jacket and tossing it over the back of a chair.

Ronnie pointed to an arched doorway. "Through there and to the left."

He noticed she didn't divest herself of her hoodie or make a move to accompany him. Cold feet? he wondered.

Stopping in front of her, he said, "Relax. I won't bite." He almost added, "Unless you want me to," but shut his mouth.

Probably best he behaved or he wouldn't be seeing the inside of her house again anytime soon. And it was a nice house. Small but comfortable. Furnished with mostly hand-me-downs, more functional than fancy. Very much Ronnie's style.

"Come on." He folded her hand inside his. "Let's sit and get to know each other better. Catch up on the last six years. I want to hear about everything you've been doing. You must have interests besides work keeping you busy. Book club. Line dancing lessons. Wine tasting."

She acquiesced, but only after he gave her a gentle tug. Nate tried not to gloat.

Luck remained on Nate's side. He wasn't sure he could convince Ronnie to sit next to him, but cardboard boxes occupied both chairs. Only the couch was empty.

"You moving?" he asked.

"Stuff from Dad I haven't had a chance to unpack yet. Dolores moved in with him this past spring. They needed room at the house for her things and have been unloading our old belongings on me and Mel and Frankie."

"Belongings like the bicycle I saw in the garage?"

"Yeah, along with ribbons and trophies and photos and scrapbooks. Like I need a poster from my third grade science fair project or my Girl Scout uniform."

"I'd like to see those."

"They're a lot less interesting than you might think."

When he plunked down on the couch, she joined him, but not before removing her hoodie and laying it over the couch arm. Progress, he told himself. She felt safe enough to forgo her customary armor.

"I have an important question for you," he asked once they were both settled, legs extended and boots resting on the leather upholstered footrest.

"What's that?"

"Did you see the poster in the bar for the Valentine's Day dance?"

She nodded thoughtfully. "I did."

"Are you going?"

"I haven't decided." Her expression quickly changed to one of alarm. "Are you asking me?"

"No, that's the day I'm not fit for company. I was simply wondering."

She reclined against the cushion, obviously relieved.

"I do have another question."

"Oh?" Alarm reappeared on her face.

"Why did you come running to see if I was okay?"

"I was concerned for your safety."

"Theo was concerned for my safety. He told me later. But he didn't send your dad down to check on me. Bess didn't come, and I'm her employee. You did, Ronnie." He inched closer. "I want to know why."

"I don't hate you, Nate. I didn't want to see you hurt."

"Everyone in the stands tonight doesn't hate me and didn't want to see me hurt. They also didn't set a fifty-meter dash record."

She glared at him, though it was a pretty wimpy glare. "You want me to admit I still care for you?"

"Do you?"

"By your own account, that was a fantastic kiss back there in the garage. I'm either an Oscar-worthy actress or I care for you. At least a little."

"It's possible to desire someone and have incredible chemistry but not like them."

"For me it isn't."

He cupped her shoulder with his palm. "Let's try it again."

She pulled back.

"If, after one kiss, you admit to caring for me at least a little, how much more will you care after two?"

"Be serious, Nate."

"I am." He bent and pressed his forehead to hers. "Want to know if I still care for you?"

Her expression became somber. "You're not exactly hiding the fact you do."

"True."

"But I hurt you once. Badly. You can't pretend it didn't happen."

"Enough of the past. Let's move forward."

Like in the garage, he stopped her from saying more with a kiss. This one, however, was filled with tenderness rather than wild hunger.

Also like before, she went soft in his arms. And without the passion clouding his senses, Nate experienced a deep emotional connection with her far exceeding any physical one.

The effect on him was ten times greater than before. He knew then he wasn't over Ronnie and had never been despite what he'd told himself and others. That was why he'd stayed in town, not because he needed answers or closure.

As the kiss continued, he felt like he couldn't live another day, another moment, without her beside him, her body nestled in the crook of his when he went to bed at night and woke in the morning.

Dangerous desires, for sure. She wasn't ready and, to be entirely honest, he wasn't, either. They really should go slow, all kidding aside, rather than ruin a potentially good thing.

He let out a long exhale when they shifted apart. "Maybe we should stop."

"I'm not sure I want that."

"You're kidding, of course." He studied her, searching for the hint of teasing. "I'm on shaky ground here and will easily take what you say the wrong way."

"That first kiss *was* fantastic." She smiled shyly. "I liked this one better."

"Why?"

"You'll think I'm silly."

"Who, me?"

"It was more romantic, and you can sometimes be a really romantic guy."

Her admission seeped inside and imprinted itself on his heart.

"I had a revelation of sorts tonight," she said.

"About?"

"You. Us." Her glance sought his. "I've missed you, Nate. Missed what we had. It was good."

"Before it went bad," he reminded her.

"Mel accused me of hiding out in Mustang Valley after I left you and trying to convince myself and everyone else that I'm happy when I'm not. She's sort of right. I haven't been happy exactly. But not unhappy, either."

"That describes me perfectly. Not happy, not unhappy."

"I like kissing you, Nate. I like sitting on the couch with you. I would probably like taking this further and heading off to the bedroom."

He forced himself not to jump to conclusions. "Didn't we just review the ground rules?"

"And nothing's changed." She twisted on the cushion to face him. "You're still wounded, deep down, and I'm still buried in grief and guilt over the miscarriage and the terrible way I treated you. Not the best combination to begin with, and sleeping together will only cause our insecurities to increase, not decrease."

"I hate it when you make good sense," he said, resigning himself to the inevitable. "And on that note, I should probably go."

She stood when he did and walked with him while he grabbed his jacket and then his hat.

"Good luck tomorrow," he said, opening his truck door. "I'll help if you need it."

She stood on tiptoes and kissed his cheek. "Good night, Nate."

Turning away from her, he touched the spot.

How was it possible? Each kiss had gotten progressively sweeter. This last one was downright innocent. But their effect on him had escalated, leaving him floundering in an emotional tidal wave. He barely remembered the drive home to The Small Change.

ANXIETY BEFORE A rodeo was nothing new to Ronnie. Today, though, her anxiety was getting the best of her. She'd snapped at Sam and was repaid with the silent treatment. Next, she'd failed to look where she was going and stubbed her toe on a student's grooming box. And perhaps the most humiliating of all, she'd burst into tears when her dad had come over to wish her luck.

Spending ten minutes in the Poco Dinero restroom composing herself had calmed her nerves. Marginally. With twenty minutes left before the barrel racing event started, she was flitting from one participant to the next, offering last-minute assistance, advice or support.

"Sorry about earlier," she told Sam.

"It's okay. Not like I haven't bitten your head off recently."

The teenager wasn't competing today, not in an official capacity. As the town's newest minor celebrity, she'd be making the first opening run on Comanche in order to excite the crowd and generate interest—for herself and for Ronnie.

Bess had agreed to not only announce a brief history of Sam's journey to Nationals, but to also mention that the horse she rode had been schooled by Ronnie, former barrel racing state champion and local horse trainer.

Fair was fair. Part of Ronnie's agreement with Bess was the opportunity to promote her school. Ronnie's list of clients and students was growing, but not in proportion to her mounting expenses.

Today just had to go well, Ronnie told herself as she checked to make sure the girth was tight on a student's horse. Too much was at stake. She had enough money to carry her for a couple more months. After that, and without an increase in revenue, the future of her school would be in jeopardy.

Board for her horses wasn't cheap. Neither was the monthly fee she paid to Powell Ranch for use of their facilities. There was also the cost of traveling to various rodeos and fairs to drum up new business. Advertising in rodeo magazines. Maintaining a website. The list went on and on.

What small salary Ronnie paid herself no longer covered the rent on her house and living expenses. She'd joked last night with Nate about finding a roommate, except she wasn't laughing today.

"You ready?"

Hearing Nate come up behind her, she dropped the stirrup on her student's saddle and gave the horse a pat on the rump. "Almost."

The girl thanked Ronnie and left to join her friends gathering outside the arena gate. Pivoting to face him, Ronnie plastered a smile on her face, hoping to convey a confidence she didn't quite feel.

He noticed immediately she wasn't herself and asked, "Are you okay?"

In response, she motioned with her hand. "There's a lot going on. As you can see."

What was the matter with her? Back in her competition days, she'd battled anxiety before an event but hadn't suffered from doubts regarding her abilities. That had come later, after her last trip to Nationals, her miscarriage and the falling out with Nate's mother.

No, not true, she realized. It had come in the weeks following her walking out on Nate.

She'd assumed that after taking a month off to clear her head, she would jump right back into competing, with plenty of time to qualify again for Nationals. Only that month had stretched into two, then three. Before she quite knew it, summer had arrived, and she was still at loose ends.

When Nate had told her about losing his drive, she hadn't shared with him her own acute loss of the very same thing. How could she admit the cause of their problems—her insistence on competing—had ceased to be important to her?

Ultimately, ironically and sadly, Ronnie had never been to a professional rodeo again, other than as a spectator and to support her students.

"You're not having second thoughts about last night, are you?" Nate asked.

"Why would I? Nothing happened."

"Okay. So much for me thinking I rocked your world." His grin deepened rather than disappeared.

"Ah. The kissing." She zipped up her hoodie. "Please don't take this the wrong way."

"Uh-oh." He pretended to brace himself.

If her nerves weren't getting the best of her, she'd have laughed. "I haven't thought about last night a whole lot. I've been too busy."

"I won't take that as an insult." He hitched his chin at the bleachers. "There's a good-size crowd."

"Yeah." Thank goodness. Ronnie had been imagining the worst, which included Bess informing her the barrel racing wasn't working out and they were canceling all future events.

"And I heard you have twenty-six entries."

"Not as many as bull riding but a respectable number." Another of her fears eliminated.

"I wanted to get here sooner. We had a small emergency this morning at the ranch."

Ronnie really should check with her other students, but his news stopped her. "What happened?"

"Theo fell."

"Is he all right?" Concern flared. Her father hadn't said anything. Then again, he didn't work today and might not have heard.

"Twisted his ankle pretty good. He wanted to be here today. Reese insisted he stay home. Keep the ankle elevated and iced."

"She's right," Ronnie concurred. "I'm glad it's nothing serious."

"Physically, no. Emotionally, that's another story. He was trying to climb on the tractor. Apparently one of the hands didn't show up this morning. Too much celebrating last night is the rumor. Theo decided to help with the morning feeding."

"Why didn't you stop him?"

"He's not normally up that early, much less out and about." Nate rubbed the back of his neck as if to relieve tension. "I feel bad for him. Reese has forbidden him to ever drive a tractor again, and I think he's taking it hard. That was something he used to do every day, and now it's one more restriction thanks to his Parkinson's. She's also insisting he see a doctor."

"And he's refusing?"

"You know Theo."

"Hey, Ronnie! Can you help me with this?" The young woman, a student of Ronnie's, struggled with the buckle on her chaps.

"Just one second."

"I didn't intend to keep you," Nate said. "Good luck today."

She turned, assuming he'd saunter off. She should have known better. The next instant, he swept her into his arms and pulled her flush against him.

"Nate," she protested when he dipped his head. "Just because I let you kiss me last night doesn't mean you can kiss me anytime you want."

"You're right," he drawled, his lips temptingly close. "Sorry."

If only she didn't like kissing him so much and find everything about him attractive. Even his take control attitude, which should annoy her, gave her a small thrill. As he held her, the thrill wound lazily through her, lighting random nerve endings along its path.

Summoning the last shred of her willpower, she said, "Please."

He released her with the same swiftness as he'd embraced her. Ronnie righted her lopsided hat and waited until her balance returned. By then, Nate had sped off in the direction of the bleachers.

"Ronnie!" the young woman with the uncooperative buckle called.

"Yeah, yeah." She brushed the front of her hoodie though not a speck of dirt clung to it.

A hug. Nate had given her a hug. No big deal. She'd been getting hugs all afternoon. No one would think anything of it. Her student hadn't noticed, and she stood ten feet away.

How was that possible? Ronnie's cheeks must certainly be flushed, given how warm they were to the touch. When she approached the student, her legs wobbled and her voice came out an octave higher. All dead giveaways Ronnie was flummoxed.

Nate did that to her. He was the only one. Ronnie considered herself rather unflappable, except, apparently, where he was concerned.

"What's the hold up?" Bess made a pass through the area, shouting and clapping her hands on her way to the announcer's booth. "Everyone ready?"

Finishing with her student, Ronnie searched for her youngest sister. Rather than chatting with her friends, Sam stood close to her boyfriend, Drew, Comanche's reins hanging loose as he nosed the ground.

"Hurry up," Ronnie called to Sam at the same moment Drew went in for a kiss.

Ronnie would have reprimanded her sister if she herself hadn't recently been in a very similar situation.

Suddenly music started to play, and Bess's voice blared from the speakers. Sam dragged herself away from Drew, climbed onto Comanche and entered the arena to a cheering crowd of a hundred-plus spectators. After making a circuit and waving, she executed a flawless run of the barrels, her time excellent for an arena that size.

Unlike the bull riding, barrel racing didn't have multiple rounds with participants advancing. Everyone got one run per horse. Some participants entered two horses. First, second and third places were determined by whoever had the best time once all the participants had gone.

The prize money wasn't as great as it was for bull riding, either, though the winners took home a decent amount for a single afternoon's work.

For the serious professional, the event was a good

opportunity to practice in a situation resembling a real rodeo. For others, it was a proving ground for untested horses. All enjoyed a fun afternoon.

At the end of the event, Ronnie accepted the congratulations of friends, family, acquaintances, clients and even strangers. She was introduced to many individuals expressing an interest in her school and passed out a small stack of business cards.

One set of parents raved about Comanche and scheduled an appointment to look at him as a potential horse for their daughter. They went so far as to offer a deposit if Ronnie agreed to hold the horse until after they'd had the chance to "test drive" him, as the father put it.

Like the previous evening, Bess invited spectators inside for reduced prices on drinks. With a two-hour wait until the bull riding started, plenty of people accepted. A collection was taken and pizzas ordered for delivery from the market.

Ronnie initially considered going home. Instead, she hung around, making even more connections as the bull riding crowd arrived. At the rate she was going, she'd have no problem recruiting enough new clients and students to increase her revenue. She might even be able to turn a decent profit sooner than expected.

Her emotions high, she went looking for Nate, wanting to share her good fortune with him. She located him at the bar, talking to a group of attractive cowgirls. They were clearly infatuated with him, smiling prettily and finding reasons to touch his hand or arm.

Ronnie tried not to be jealous. She had no claim on Nate despite the kisses they'd shared. In fact, she'd gone out of her way to discourage him. She should have expected something like this.

He noticed her at the same moment she decided to

leave, and his expression brightened. Saying something she couldn't hear, he abandoned the cowgirls and came toward her.

"Did I interrupt?" Ronnie asked, trying to tamp down her sarcasm.

"Wish I could stay, but duty calls." With a quick good-bye and see you later, he headed outside.

No hug? Well, she had warned him.

Ronnie assured herself she wasn't bothered by his abrupt departure or the gaggle of cowgirls. From then on, she managed only glimpses of him. When her family returned for the bull riding, she postponed going home and joined them in the stands.

There was no mishap at the bucking chutes like before or any other calamity to send her hurrying to Nate's side. About as many people showed up as the previous evening, some new, some repeats. Ronnie had heard Bess was anticipating an increase in attendance as time went on. Ronnie hoped so, too, what with her, Nate and Bess all standing to benefit.

There was no reason for her to remain and talk to Nate when the bull riding ended. She'd congratulated him on the event last night. But her spirits still soared from her potential good news, and she wanted to tell him. What harm was there in that?

"Did he go home?" she asked one of The Small Change hands after scouring the entire premises twice.

"No idea."

The guy was obviously more interested in his neighbor on the next bar stool over, a saucy looking woman in tight jeans and definitely not from Mustang Valley.

Disheartened, Ronnie opted to leave. It was late. Her family had long gone. She had a lot to do the following day and needed her sleep. Besides, it was entirely possible Nate hadn't left alone.

At the first intersection, she stopped, letting her truck idle. To the left was home. To the right, The Small Change ranch and Nate. Drawing in a deep breath, she swung the steering wheel to the right.

Chapter Ten

Sliding out of her truck, Ronnie slammed the door shut behind her. The sound was unnaturally loud in the dark, eerie stillness of the ranch.

Had she ever been here this late at night before? A few times as a child, when her father had had an emergency and she and her sisters had been too young to stay home by themselves.

She'd been spooked back then, too, seeing the ranch cloaked in shadows rather than bathed in sunlight. In the distance, owls hooted, dogs barked and horses shifted in their stalls. At a coyote's high-pitched yipping, Ronnie's skin prickled. Silly, of course. She heard coyotes all the time.

Must be her elevated emotions making her edgy. But now that she'd left the bar and the music and the noisy, excited crowd, second thoughts assailed her.

"What are you doing here?" she asked on a whisper. "Are you crazy?"

There was no chance Nate would interpret her appearance at his trailer as anything other than a wish on her part to take their relationship to the next level, whatever that might be. Hanging out. Dating. Commitment.

Was that what she wanted? If not, she should hightail it out of here this very moment before he saw her. He must have heard her truck approach and possibly spotted the headlights from his window.

His curtained window, she noted. And though a low light burned from within, there'd been no sign of movement. Perhaps he wasn't home. He could be out with one of the cowgirls from the bar. Or, she could be inside with him, the two of them buried beneath the covers.

The jealousy from earlier returned, coiling around her chest and squeezing.

"This is stupid," she hissed. "You're acting like a child."

She jerked when the door to the trailer's living quarters opened.

"Ronnie?"

A flashlight beam climbed her body to her face, and she raised a hand to shield her eyes from the glare.

"Did I wake you?" she asked in a squeaky voice.

"What are you doing here? It's late."

Was he alone? She squinted and tried to see past him and inside.

"I, ah…"

Great. What had struck her as a good idea twenty minutes ago now seemed pathetic and immature. What was she? A stalker? A Peeping Tom?

"I looked for you earlier," she finally said, glad the squeak was gone. "At the Poco Dinero. You'd left."

"I figured I'd check on Theo after his fall." Nate lowered the flashlight. "Is everything all right?"

"Yeah. Sure. I… I…you'd left," she repeated her same feeble statement.

As her eyes adjusted, the details came slowly into focus. Nate wore jeans and a western-cut shirt. No boots, no socks, no belt. The shirt was unbuttoned and hung open, revealing a good portion of his chest. His well-toned chest, she might add.

Wasn't he cold? Evidently not, for he leaned a shoulder against the door frame in a classically sexy pose that was very much Nate. The old Nate, at least. Easy, confident and amused rather than frustrated and disappointed with the world around him. The Nate she'd fallen in love with and might have spent her life with if unfortunate circumstances and bad decision making hadn't conspired against them.

He didn't invite her inside, she noticed. Maybe there really was a woman in there with him!

"How is Theo?" Ronnie asked. "Any better?"

Why wasn't she leaving? Had she lost every bit of her good sense?

"He's sporting a bruised right arm and a sprained ankle. Reese is worried, but Theo refuses to see his doctor or go to the emergency medical clinic tomorrow. He insists it's nothing."

"What do you think?"

"He's a tough old guy. The injuries won't kill him, but he could probably use some prescription pain relievers and maybe an X-ray of the ankle just to be on the safe side."

Ronnie nodded, and an awkward silence fell between them like heavy fog.

"Well, I suppose—"

She didn't have a chance to finish, a melodic ding interrupting her.

"Wait here." He disappeared inside. A moment passed and he returned, his cell phone in his hand. Finishing typing, he set the phone on the counter beside him. The bemused expression he'd been wearing had vanished.

"What's wrong?" Only when the question was out did she remember Nate's business was none of hers.

"That was my mom." He resumed leaning on the doorjamb. "She called before you got here and apparently forgot to tell me something."

"Ah." Refusing to let another awkward silence engulf them, she said, "All good, I hope?"

"Other than her fighting off the flu." He shifted, adjusting his weight. "I told her about us."

"Us?" *Is there an us?* That and a hundred other questions sprang to mind. Ronnie couldn't sort through them fast enough.

"I said we were working together."

"Uh, yeah. Of course."

The bemusement was back in his eyes. He'd known what she was thinking. As usual. She really should work on being less predictable.

"Mom still feels terrible about what she said that night in the hospital and for the problems she caused us."

"It was hardly her fault and not the reason I left. You did tell her that, yes?"

He lifted a shoulder.

"Nate," Ronnie said with exasperation. "She was upset. We were all upset."

"Are you saying she didn't hurt you with her cruel remarks?"

"Cruel is a strong word. Maybe inconsiderate."

"Don't forget selfish."

"What does it matter now?"

He didn't answer and raked his fingers through his hair, leaving it slightly mussed and very attractive. "I did mention you were doing well, so I doubt she'll be losing any sleep tonight."

She appreciated his anger on her behalf but wished he'd let go of his resentment. "Tell her there's no hard feelings the next time you talk."

"We'll see." He stepped back and inclined his head to the side. "You want to come in?"

He didn't qualify the invitation with, "Just to talk," or

"To put your feet up," like he had last night at her house. From the size of his living quarters, she doubted there'd be much room for sitting and putting up their feet—which immediately conjured images of where he slept. A bunk most likely, in the area over the hitch. Not unlike the camper she used when she was traveling to rodeos.

For crying out loud, what was wrong with her? He'd asked if she wanted to come in, and she'd immediately begun pondering where he slept.

Did he have something in mind besides talking?

Who wouldn't? She'd shown up on his doorstep at eleven at night, admitting she'd tracked him down after discovering he'd left early. Given their increasing attraction and constant falling into each other's arms, naturally he'd concluded she wanted more than a casual conversation.

Ronnie could have kicked herself. This idea to surprise him had been harebrained from the start and was quickly worsening. Or was it?

In that moment, she realized she was facing a crossroads. The kind of crossroads that came around only rarely in a person's life. Whatever she did, stay or go, would impact the rest of her life. And Nate's. Their families, too.

This might be the long awaited chance to set right what had gone terribly wrong. It could also be the biggest mistake she'd ever make.

"If I come in," she stated slowly, "how possible is it that things will progress?"

One corner of his mouth curved up in a sexy grin. "What things?"

"You know." Of course he did. He was teasing her. She swallowed before replying. "Intimate things."

"Is that what we're calling them now?"

Forget the cold. Ronnie was suddenly burning up and yanked down the zipper of her hoodie. "I need to be sure."

"That you won't get hurt again?" He shook his head. "I can't guarantee it. I tried before and look what happened."

"I understand the risks." He wasn't in a position to offer her a happily-ever-after. She wasn't in a position to offer him one, either. But as long as they were both cautious, they should be okay. "I need to be sure you…you… care for me." Admitting her vulnerability wasn't easy.

"You said yourself I've been clear on that."

"You might have been joking."

"All right, then. Let me set the record straight." Nate grabbed a handhold and lowered himself onto the ground. Her heart kicked into high gear as he advanced. "If you come inside with me, and, trust me, I hope you do, there will be intimate things happening. Lots of them."

She sucked in a soft gasp when he came to a stop in front of her, the tails of his open shirt fluttering in the breeze, the pure masculine sight and scent of him having a dizzying effect on her equilibrium.

"I, um, see."

"And the reason there will be intimate things is because I care about you. A great deal, Ronnie. That's the only reason. If I didn't, I'd send you packing."

"I…yeah." Her jaw had gone slack, making speech difficult.

"If you aren't ready—" his hands captured her upper arms and squeezed "—if this isn't want you want—" he bent and brushed his lips across hers "—then you'd best skedaddle."

Skedaddle? Wasn't that the word she'd used on his first day back in Mustang Valley?

"No pressure," he added. "You need a minute to decide?" His drawl rolled over her as he found her neck and nibbled lightly. "Or a little more convincing?"

She held on to him in an effort to steady herself against the assault of sensations.

"Ronnie?" He tugged on her ear with his teeth.

"I'm ready." A shiver of anticipation quickened her pulse. "Take me inside."

"Nope." He released her and backed away. "This is something you have to do yourself."

Ronnie nodded, comprehending. The decision must be entirely hers.

Sending him a radiant smile, she said, "Follow me," and walked toward the trailer, leaving behind all her doubts and insecurities.

She was here. Alone with him. He'd been fantasizing about this very moment for days. Weeks. Okay, years.

Contrary to what Nate claimed, he hadn't ever gotten over Ronnie. If that were so, he'd have been with other woman. There'd been opportunities, with genuinely nice gals he'd met during his travels and those looking for a brief escape in the dark with a warm, willing body.

He'd turned all but a few of them down for different reasons. When he'd tried dating, the end result was inevitably injured or angry feelings. Eventually, he'd stopped trying. What he hadn't known then and did now was he'd been waiting for Ronnie and this night.

Slow. He must not forget to go slow, resist the urge to hurry. It wouldn't be easy, but it would be worth the effort. He'd make sure of that.

She stood facing him in the small space between the cabinets and the two-seater table, close enough he could see the irises of her upturned eyes changing from green to almost gold.

"What next?"

A dozen suggestions filled his mind. "That's up to you."

"I suppose we should get undressed. There isn't much room in the bunk for that."

The grin he'd been holding back erupted on his face. "Excellent idea." Stripping off his shirt, he tossed it into a corner.

When he paused, she said, "Keep going."

Oh, yeah. This was going to be good. "Tell me when to stop."

Unzipping his jeans, he stepped out of them. The limp heap landed on top of his shirt. When he was done, he squared his shoulders. Only his boxer briefs remained.

With deliberate movements, he hooked his thumbs in the waistband.

"Wait." Ronnie's gaze on him was unwavering.

He lowered the briefs an inch. "For what?"

"I need to catch up." She shrugged off her hoodie.

Forget good, this was going to be fantastic. He watched her remove each article of clothing, one by one and in her own sweet time. They all ended up in the pile he'd started with his clothes.

"You're killing me, you know," he said when she stood in just her bra and panties.

And what bra and panties they were. Peach colored, sheer in the most interesting places and a shade deeper than the abundance of gorgeous skin she'd exposed. Staring openly, he gulped, attempting to moisten his parched throat.

"You are so beautiful," he said, marveling at the sight of her.

She blushed. When had she ever done that? The color

spread from her cheeks to her neck to her the lovely tops of her breasts peeking out from the bra.

"Still full of compliments," she chided him.

"I mean every one."

When she reached behind her to unhook the bra, he stopped her. "Allow me."

A small smile touched her lips. "All right."

She turned and presented her back. With unsteady hands, he unfastened the hooks and let the bra fall to the floor. Turning her in the circle of his arms, he folded her in his embrace.

The contact was electric, and he went hard with desire. She had to notice but rather than pull away or stiffen, she melted against him and sighed contentedly.

"Ronnie." With one hand, he removed the clip securing her ponytail. When her long locks were free, he swept them aside and nuzzled her neck.

"Yes," she murmured.

"I want to make this as special for you as possible."

"I'd like that, too."

"This next part, well, there's not much I can do. It's going to be clumsy."

She did stiffen then. "Tell me."

"Better I show you."

Stooping slightly, he caught her behind the knees with one arm while supporting her back with the other. Straightening, he held her like one might a small child or, he couldn't help thinking, a groom carrying his bride over the threshold.

"What are you doing?" she demanded.

Instead of answering her, he raised her high and deposited her onto the bunk. She bounced once before settling.

"Scoot over," he said. "Make room for me."

She complied, laughing and scrambling to the far side as he hoisted himself up to join her. When he landed on the mattress, it gave beneath his weight, and she bounced again. This time, he joined in her laughter.

They both quieted when he rolled on top and pinned her beneath him. Those green-gold eyes of hers darkened with desire.

"This isn't just sex," he said, surprised at the shaky quality of his voice.

"For me, either."

"I want you. Don't get me wrong."

Her playful smile returned. "I can tell."

"Yeah. Well, you've always had that effect on me, sweetheart. Can't be helped."

"Same here. And once we get the rest of these clothes off, you'll see for yourself."

Neither of them were shy, and they'd had a satisfying sex life at one time, fueled by their adventurous natures and active imaginations. He didn't think either of them had changed despite their limited partners and long stretches of abstinence.

"I really like your panties." He shifted and tugged on the elastic band. "Get rid of them."

Issuing a throaty chuckle, she elevated her behind, allowing him to drag the flimsy piece of fabric down the length of her body. She assisted with the last stubborn inches, kicking the panties off.

Pausing to examine his handiwork, he uttered a sound of satisfaction. "That's better."

"I agree. Except for this." She tugged on the waistband of his boxer briefs.

Nate couldn't remove them fast enough and bumped his head on the roof of the trailer in the process.

"Careful," Ronnie warned, humor lightening her voice.

Both of them naked at last, he lay beside her and nestled her close. Starting at her knee, he slid his palm up her thigh, skimmed it over her tummy and continued until it came to rest on one full, pliant breast. Then, lowering his head, he breathed deeply before drawing a delicate nipple into his mouth.

This was what he'd missed the most. Not just the sex, but the sight of her exquisite and lithe form, the heady scent of her skin and the delectable taste of her.

"Ronnie." He held back, willing the moment to last.

She arched into him, small moans escaping her lips. "Hurry."

"No way." He continued his exploration of her body. "I've been away a long time. I need to get my bearings first."

"Is that just an excuse to extend foreplay?" She stretched languidly.

"Got me figured out, have you?"

"You're going to have to make the wait worthwhile."

He raised himself on one elbow and grinned down at her. "Challenge accepted."

"And then it's my turn."

"Even better."

He did his best to please her—and succeeded, more than once. She was incredible to watch, her face taking on a rapturous expression and her skin glowing with a faint flush. He didn't need to remember what she liked, he'd never forgotten.

When she'd attempted to satisfy him in return, he refused her, saying, "Not yet. First I want to…"

"What?" she murmured.

"This."

Nudging her legs apart, he let his fingers explore. Tantalize. Delight. She held him when she peaked and called his name. Afterward, he cradled her close and pressed his lips to hers. Feeling tears on her cheeks, he drew back.

"Are you crying?"

"No." She sniffed.

"Why?" He brushed her mussed hair away from her face.

"Emotional overload. There's a lot happening in my heart right now. Crying helps me process it."

He could buy that. A lot was happening in his heart, too, that needed processing. "What can I do?"

"I'm fine, really." She snuggled closer. "Just give me a minute."

He did, running his fingers up and down her arm in what he hoped was a soothing gesture. Before long, she turned into him. Nate was content at calling it a night. Ronnie's satisfaction mattered more to him than his own.

She, however, had other plans and wrapped her fingers around his still-full erection. There was no stopping the groan that started low in his throat. She'd always had the silkiest of touches and a keen ability to predict his reactions.

Nate reached the point of no return far sooner than he would have liked. "Not yet." The words tore from his throat.

"I could—"

Pulling her on top of him, he positioned her so that she straddled his middle. Right where he wanted her. "You're incredible," he said as she guided him inside her.

The sensation was immediate and all consuming. Nate didn't resist. He couldn't. He *wouldn't.*

With the bunk's low ceiling Ronnie had to lean low over him, a position that brought her lips and breasts tantalizingly close. He kissed her with a passion denied for six long years. She responded by moving her hips and squeezing with her thighs.

He and Ronnie had made love often. But this was different. They were hungrier. Needier. Perhaps their long separation was responsible. Or the undecided state of their future. Risk did add an element of excitement.

"Touch me," she said, her voice urgent.

"Try to stop me." He ran his hands down her slim back and farther, over the soft, rounded curves and smooth plains of her body.

Delaying the inevitable became impossible when Ronnie surrendered to another shattering climax. He dived over the edge after her, losing a piece of himself as he did and knowing he'd find it in the recesses of her heart, next to all the other pieces of himself he'd lost to her.

They lay quiet for several long minutes, arms and legs entwined, breathing slowing at the same rate. If Nate could hear Ronnie's heart beating, he was sure the rhythm of his own would match. They were that much in sync.

Soon, too soon in his opinion, she tried to extract herself. "I should probably leave."

"Don't." His arm circled her shoulders, and he pulled her back down. "Spend the night with me."

"What will Reese think? She might not like you having overnight guests."

"I'll quit my job if it comes to that."

"Be serious," Ronnie said, though she didn't attempt to move away.

"I'm pretty sure Reese won't mind. It's not as if we're running naked through the ranch and corrupting innocent children. Though, if you want to run around naked in a more secluded place, I think that might be fun."

She rolled her eyes and shook her head.

"Stay, Ronnie." He shifted so that they were face-to-face, his eyes locked with hers. "I want to wake up with you here beside me."

Her expression softened. "We can't re-create the past."

"Who wants that? Not me. Personally, I'm looking toward the future. We were both damaged by what happened, enough that we threw away what was, for me anyway, the best thing in my life. Neither of us can change that. But we've grown since then. Learned. Healed a little. In your case, you know what you want in life. I'm still working on that part, but I've made a start."

"How can we be sure we won't repeat our mistakes?"

"How can we be sure of anything? But I know I don't want to continue the way I have been, refusing to put down roots or hold a job for more than a couple months."

She remained silent for several moments.

He kissed the top of her head. "Don't overthink this. Not tonight, at least. Tomorrow, we can analyze the heck out of each other."

"Let me think about it."

In the end, she stayed with Nate. He swore it wouldn't be the last time, that he'd do whatever Ronnie wanted, whatever was required to continue this fresh start they'd been given.

There were still obstacles ahead of them, problems to solve and old issues to be resolved. Nothing would change overnight. But if they were both willing to put in the effort, they just might have a chance.

Chapter Eleven

Nate came gradually awake, feeling cramped and crowded. His entire left arm was numb from lack of circulation. He didn't care. Ronnie lay tucked beside him, warm and lush and…was she snoring?

No, not snoring. More like a delicate snuffling sound as she shifted in her sleep. Very cute.

She moved again, this time letting up a bit on the pressure to his arm. A thousand needles stabbed him as blood flow returned. Clamping his teeth together, he stifled a groan and waited until the intense sensation passed, not wanting to disturb her. She looked so content and slumbered so peacefully in the gray half-light of his trailer.

They'd finally fallen asleep last night a little past midnight by Nate's estimation. The long day, their incredible lovemaking and the emotional conversations before and after had taken a toll on them, and they'd both fallen into a deep sleep. That had been about six hours ago, according to the clock on Nate's microwave. He would have to get out of bed soon and head over to the ranch house to assist Theo with his morning routine—which would certainly be affected by his fall yesterday and sprained ankle.

If Reese had managed to convince her father to see a doctor, Nate intended to offer his assistance.

"You awake?" Ronnie murmured and turned beneath the covers in order to face him, a sleepy smile on her lips.

"Yeah. Just." He dropped a light kiss on her forehead and drew her nearer. "I hope you weren't too cold."

"Mmm. Not at all."

"I don't like leaving the electric heater on while I sleep. Too much of a fire hazard."

"You kept me perfectly toasty."

"Good." Neither of them wore any clothes, and he'd worried the blankets weren't heavy enough.

She draped a leg over his and sighed. He very much liked the sensation of her smooth skin caressing his.

"I suppose I should get going."

"You don't have to," he insisted, adjusting his own leg to allow for more contact.

"I'd rather not hang around too long. My dad is the livestock foreman here, and employees have big mouths."

Nate didn't argue with her. Only a skeleton crew worked on Sundays, but they might recognize Ronnie's truck and report back to her dad. She was entitled to tell her family what she chose when she chose. She shouldn't be forced into a position of explaining herself because they'd been careless.

If she wanted him with her when she told her family, he'd gladly oblige. That, too, was Ronnie's call.

"Can I talk you into a shower first?" he asked, hopping down from the bunk. Moving quickly in the cold air, he switched on a light and rummaged through the pile of clothes they'd left on the floor for his jeans and shirt.

"I'll wait till I get home. Your shower's really small. I'm surprised you fit."

He immediately imagined him and Ronnie crammed together in the tiny space, their bodies wet and soapy. The fantasy was an appealing one and something he'd like to try in the future.

"Let me make you a cup of coffee for the road at least," he said.

Ronnie sat up as high as she could in the bunk, her head touching the ceiling. "That sounds great."

He helped her down and handed over her clothes.

"Brrr." She pretended to shiver. Or, maybe she wasn't pretending. "It's cold in here."

"Living in a trailer isn't for the faint of heart." Nate plugged in the portable heater and set the temperature to high.

"Do you ever miss four walls and central heating?"

"Sure." He slipped on his socks and then buttoned his shirt. "Not enough to settle down before now."

She paused in the middle of zipping her hoodie. "Are you saying your wandering days are over?"

"Possibly. That depends."

Her hands fell away from the half-zipped hoodie. "Look. I realize we spent the night together and that might give you reason to jump to certain assumptions."

"Don't worry, I'm not making any assumptions," he said before she could warn him they weren't picking up where they'd left off years ago. "But I do have one expectation I insist on, and it's big."

One lovely arched eyebrow rose. "What's that?"

"I want to see you again, Ronnie."

"See me? Like a date?"

"We'll call it that. As long as, at some point, we sit or walk together, holding hands as we discuss where this, us, is heading."

"When?" She finished zipping her hoodie, not looking at him.

"Later this week? Tuesday? Whenever you're free. You name the day." He went over to her, hooked a finger beneath her chin and tilted her face up. "I'm not expecting a repeat of last night. Not until you're ready, anyway. Your call. Of course I want that, don't get me wrong. It was incredible. But I can wait. Hell, I've waited nearly six years."

"Tuesday's good," she answered softly.

"Would you like to go to dinner?" He'd almost said lunch, not wanting to remind them both of their last dinner out on Valentine's Day.

"Okay."

"Is it?" He wished he sounded more confident.

"Yes." Her tender smile lit him up inside.

While she washed her face and combed her hair in the small bathroom, Nate made them both coffee. He fixed hers in a travel mug, which he insisted she take with her and return later.

Outside, he walked her to her truck. Making sure no one was in the vicinity to see them, he gave her a combination good morning and goodbye kiss that left him aching for more.

Returning to the trailer after she drove off, he finished his coffee, made the bed and took a quick shower. After that, he checked on Breeze before starting toward the house. Enrico's nephew was driving the tractor in the east pasture, delivering a flatbed trailer of hay to the horses. Nate couldn't help thinking that was the job Theo had been attempting when he fell.

Nate was pretty sure his feet weren't entirely touching the ground during the quarter-mile stroll. It was hard not to feel good after the last twenty-four hours and look forward to the future. Still, he resisted getting too far ahead of himself.

He was a realist and wouldn't ignore the challenges he and Ronnie faced. On the other hand, he couldn't help counting the factors in his favor: being gainfully employed, having a place to live—if not truly a home— meeting people he was starting to consider his friends, making a small contribution to Sam qualifying for Nationals and, best of all, having an upcoming dinner date with Ronnie.

The door to the kitchen stood ajar, and he went in. Flora was there to greet him, bustling about as she prepared a breakfast of pancakes and bacon.

"Morning, ma'am. Smells good in here." Nate removed his cowboy hat. "Theo up yet?"

The housekeeper frowned worriedly. "Señor McGraw and Señora Dempsey are in the living room."

"Is Theo okay?" Nate wondered if the older man's injuries had worsened during the night.

"I do not know." She held her hands out in surrender. "He says he is fine. Señora Dempsey, she wants him to visit the doctor."

Nate wasn't sure if he should interrupt Theo and Reese or leave them alone to work out their differences. The next instant, the decision was made for him.

"Nate, is that you?" Theo hollered from the living room.

"Yes, sir."

"Come in here, will you?"

Whatever Reese said in reply, Nate couldn't hear. He glanced at Flora, who shook her head dismally and went back to cooking.

"Hurry up," Theo hollered again.

Nate exited the kitchen and crossed the wide entry way to the living room, his boots echoing on the hardwood floor only to be muffled the next second by thick area rugs. Theo wore his bathrobe and sat at the wet bar, which struck Nate as a bit odd, considering he wasn't supposed to drink and certainly not at this early hour.

Reese occupied an easy chair near the bar. Visibly

tense, she gripped the chair arms while her left leg beat a fast tattoo.

"How are you feeling this morning?" Nate asked, approaching Theo.

"Fit as a fiddle."

"He is not," Reese insisted. "His arm is black and blue, his ankle is swollen to twice its normal size and he's been having dizzy spells."

Theo shot her an angry frown. "You mind if I talk to my caregiver myself?"

Reese stood. "Nate, please tell him he should see his doctor."

"I'm not letting you drive me to the emergency room," Theo countered, "which is where we'd wind up on a Sunday as his office is closed."

"Dad." Reese's voice wobbled. "Quit being so stubborn. What if you broke a bone or tore a ligament?"

"She's not wrong, Mr. McGraw," Nate said. "I can see from here that ankle is a mess. Why don't I take you to the clinic in town? Just for a checkup. We can stop on the way back and watch Sam practice, if you want and Reese doesn't object."

"Won't work this time, young man." Theo slammed a hand onto the wet bar. "I'm not a child you can manipulate with bribes."

Since Nate had indeed been trying to bribe Theo, he didn't argue. "Will the nurse come here? Make a house call?"

"No." Reese swung around, her eyes alight. "But that new concierge doctor in north Scottsdale will. I have her business card." She started to leave only to turn back around. "Thanks, Nate. You gave me a good idea."

"I didn't say yes," Theo called after her.

She either didn't hear him or chose not to listen.

"Dammit, Nate," Theo grumbled. "I thought you were on my side."

"I am. And by that I mean I'm on the side that keeps you healthy and safe." He went over and placed a hand on Theo's back. "Reese is right. Let the doctor look at your arm and ankle. It won't kill you."

His shoulders slumped. "She's going to tell me I can't go outside anymore. Refuse to leave me alone for a minute. Before you got here, she found me in the courtyard and gave me a chewing out."

"Sneaking one of your cigars again?"

"She has a fit if I light up in the house. She has a fit if I light up at all. A man's entitled to at least one vice. Builds character." They both chuckled at his joke, but the next moment, Theo sobered. "I hate this damn disease."

"Beats the heck out of the other option." Nate was thinking about Allan, whose life had been cut far too short. "You want to be around long enough to see your grandchildren grow up. If you take care of yourself, you will."

The beginnings of a smile appeared on his wizened face, though it was a sad smile. "You're the only one who doesn't sugarcoat things with me. I like that about you."

"I like you, too, sir."

Reese reappeared, wearing a victory smile. "I reached the doctor. She'll be here at ten thirty."

Theo braced his hand on the bar and struggled to a standing position. "Well, come on, Nate. If I'm going to be meeting a lady doctor, you'd best help me get gussied up."

AN HOUR LATER, Reese stopped Nate in the kitchen on his way out.

"You have a minute?" she asked.

"Absolutely."

While helping Theo shower, Nate had decided to stop by the Poco Dinero before Sam's afternoon practice. With Ronnie, staying in Mustang Valley, and earning more money being his three new priorities, he had an idea or two to bounce off Bess for ways to expand on the rodeo events. She wouldn't arrive at the bar for another few hours, which gave him plenty of time for Reese.

"Can I get you a cup of coffee?" she asked, already reaching for a mug from the stack by the coffee maker.

"No, thanks. But help yourself. I've had my limit of caffeine for the morning."

"Oh. Okay." Reese hesitated, appearing uncertain of her next move. After a moment, she gestured toward the table. "What's Dad up to?"

"Sitting in the courtyard, reading the paper."

Nate joined her at the table. Flora had made herself scarce after their breakfast. When he added that to Reese suddenly wanting to talk to him, her being upset about Theo's fall and obvious nervousness, he felt convinced something was wrong. But what?

"Should Dad be out there alone?" Reese glanced toward the front of the house as if she could see through walls.

"He's not smoking a cigar. I swear."

Her smile was weak. Nate's stomach tightened.

"He has his cell phone with him. And I made sure he took his emergency alert. It's on the side table."

Reese nodded approvingly. "That's good."

Theo refused to wear the remote alert device around his neck, but with a little arm twisting, he could be convinced to keep it handy.

Nate was about to add there wasn't much trouble for Theo to get into while reading the paper, but changed his mind. Hadn't Theo snuck off yesterday and hijacked the tractor when no one was looking?

"You know what a great job I think you're doing with Dad." Reese spoke with a measured tone.

"I enjoy working with him, and I mean it."

"After yesterday, I'm concerned that a caregiver ten or fifteen hours a week just isn't enough. He needs someone twenty-four/seven. Someone with more qualifications."

Nate's apprehension increased.

"I realize when I hired you I said it didn't matter that you weren't accredited. Unfortunately, I'm starting to wonder if I made a mistake."

"I see."

Reese continued talking. What Nate heard was her telling him in the kindest way possible that he was being let go, and his spirits, so high an hour ago, promptly sank. He should have known the job here was too good to last. Fate had been giving him swift kicks for too long to start giving him a boost.

"I can stay until you find a replacement," he said quietly.

"Dad probably won't like it. He's grown quite fond of you. Me, too."

"No, ma'am, he won't."

She rested her folded hands on the table. "I'd hire you full-time, if you were available and if you were a nurse."

"Right."

"His condition is only going to worsen."

"I understand."

She blinked, and Nate saw tears in her eyes. "It's so hard, seeing him lose his abilities little by little every day. You can't imagine."

"Actually, I can."

"Of course. Your brother. I apologize for insulting

you. That just slipped out. I've been an emotional wreck since he fell. It could have been so much worse. What if he develops a blood clot?"

"You have to do what's best for your father."

Nate heard himself uttering all the right words, the words Reese wanted to and needed to hear. With each one, his spirits continued to sink. What would he tell Ronnie? Hadn't he just bragged to her last night how he was starting to get his life together? And now this.

Fortunately, he still had his job at the Poco Dinero. And he'd need that, too, as he'd likely be looking for another place to park his trailer and accommodations for Breeze. Reese had no reason to let him stay at The Small Change if he wasn't earning his keep.

Ronnie had an empty stall at her house. She loved Breeze and would gladly board the horse. Nate dismissed that idea the second after it occurred to him. He and Ronnie weren't there yet in their relationship, though she'd probably offer once she learned he'd lost his job.

When Reese finally wound down, Nate assured her not to worry, and he'd do whatever she needed of him to accomplish a smooth transition.

"I'm calling a nursing service first thing tomorrow," she said. "The concierge doctor may have a recommendation. That really was a great suggestion you made, Nate."

Not that great, apparently, or he'd still be employed.

He stumbled from the kitchen in a daze. With time to kill before he drove to the Poco Dinero, he fetched Breeze from the pasture, gave her a good brushing and worked her briefly in the round pen for a little exercise.

On any other day, he'd have enjoyed the beautiful, cool weather and putting the old mare through her paces. Instead, he struggled to stay positive.

Perhaps he should stop by the market on his way to

the bar. On a previous visit he'd noticed a bulletin board with various postings, including jobs. It was worth checking out.

When he was done exercising Breeze, he walked her twice around the grounds to cool her down before returning her to the pasture. He didn't bother calling the bar to make sure Bess was there, choosing instead to take his chances. On impulse, he purchased a dozen breakfast pastries at the market, telling himself he might need help softening up Bess.

Besides running his idea for bull riding lessons by her, he intended to press her for more details on how much money the rodeo events had made. Her vague remark from Friday night bothered him. More now, in the wake of his talk with Reese.

His timing couldn't be better. Bess was in the office tallying the previous night's proceeds with her assistant manager, Elena, when he arrived.

The door was open, but he knocked on the wooden jamb to get their attention. "Morning, boss. Elena. How goes it? Am I interrupting?"

Both of them glanced up, and Bess broke into a wide grin. "Morning to you, too. What brings you here on your day off? Figured you'd be home resting up. You certainly worked hard enough."

"I could say the same about you two." He stepped inside and held out the box of pastries. "Have you eaten yet?"

Bess's eyes gleamed like those of a small child. "Is that a bribe?"

"Of course not."

Bess and Elena exchanged conspiratorial glances. "What do you want, Nate?" Humor filled Bess's voice as she took the box and lifted the lid.

He waited until both women had oohed and aahed over the contents and made their selections.

"I was wondering how successful our first weekend was."

"You saw yourself the stands were well over ninety-percent capacity both nights and eighty-percent for Saturday afternoon's barrel racing." She wiped powdered sugar off her mouth with a napkin. "You know entries for the rodeo events were enough to cover expenses because I told you that already."

He reached for an apple turnover, wishing she'd be more specific. "Wouldn't the stands filled to a hundred-percent capacity and more entries be better?"

"Well, sure. But people stuck around for drinks, and the bar made money hand over fist. Just what I wanted."

Not, however, the rodeo events. They'd only broken even.

Bess had mentioned the possibility of a future bonus for Nate when she hired him. He doubted that would come out of bar proceeds.

She must have read something on his face for she said, "Be patient, Nate. Every new venture takes time to turn a profit. There are a lot of costs besides labor and rental of the bulls. Insurance premiums alone are enough to break me. And the monthly payments on my small business loan to construct the arena take a huge chunk out of my revenues."

"Guess I hadn't thought about that."

"Your job's safe as long as we fill the stands and have enough participants," she assured him.

Safe. That was a relief. But the job was only part-time and with no bonus or benefits. Not for a while, anyway. Nate needed something more if he hoped to make a decent living.

"Hey, you okay?"

Bess's question penetrated the fog surrounding him. "Yeah. Just thinking, have you ever considered bull riding lessons?" He told her about a place in Texas he'd visited once that offered lessons to novices.

"Huh. Interesting. Might be something we can consider down the road."

Down the road didn't help Nate with his current employment problem.

"By the way," Bess said, "did Ronnie ever find you last night? She was asking around for you."

"She did." He ignored the twinkles in Bess's and Elena's eyes. "We're going to put our heads together and come up with ways to get more participants."

"Aren't you two being proactive? I love it."

They chatted a while longer. Nate tried to hide his disappointment—this had been the first weekend after all. Bess might be singing an entirely different tune if future weekends were equally, or more, successful. She was simply exercising caution and not getting carried away. He respected her for that.

"You want to take these with you?" She held out the box of remaining pastries when he said he was leaving.

"Naw. You keep them."

"I'll get fat as a house."

He thought that unlikely. She didn't top five feet or weigh over ninety-five pounds.

"See you tomorrow, Bess. Elena."

"Make it Tuesday," Bess said. "If there's any reason for you to be here before then, I'll call."

That left Nate without work for a full two days, other than helping with Theo while waiting for the new nurse to start. And Reese didn't pay him for that. His wages were board for him and Breeze.

Outside, bright sunshine greeted him from a brilliant blue sky. His spirits, unfortunately, continued to linger somewhere around his knees. He couldn't knock the feeling he was right back where he'd been when he arrived in town, broke and with limited prospects. While not entirely true, he couldn't convince himself otherwise.

If not for Ronnie, and them spending last night together, he'd consider moving on. Then again, he really didn't know where the two of them stood, other than that they'd be having a dinner date on Tuesday involving hand-holding and conversation. What if he broadened his job search and looked for work outside Mustang Valley? He might have to—there'd been nothing but pet sitting, being a teacher's aide for the local preschool and housecleaning jobs posted on the market bulletin board.

Nate still didn't have a solid plan in place when he arrived at Powell Ranch for Sam's practice. Ronnie and Sam were already there. He spotted Ronnie standing by her truck, her phone glued to her ear. She gave him a quick wave and then went right back to her call. Sam was leisurely circling the arena on Big John, getting him to use the injured leg without putting a strain on it.

Spotting him, she walked the horse over to the fence where he stood. "You are coming with us to Las Vegas this weekend, aren't you?"

They were leaving Wednesday and staying through till Monday. Longer if Sam did well and advanced.

"I don't know, kiddo," Nate said. "There's the bull riding events."

"But you can get the time off, right? Someone will cover for you."

"It's only the second week. I hate leaving Bess without a manager this soon. That's a lot for her to handle."

Both of his employers had indicated they'd work

around his schedule if Sam qualified for Nationals. In the wake of his declining prospects, however, he was less inclined to force the issue. Though, if Reese found an immediate replacement for him, that job might not be a conflict.

"Don't get your hopes up, Sam. I do have a responsibility." Even if he did find full-time employment elsewhere, he hoped to keep working for Bess on the weekends.

"Nate," Sam whined, "you promised."

"I said I'd try. And, besides, someone has to cover for Ronnie at Saturday's barrel racing." He could definitely use the extra hours of paid work.

"I can't win without you."

The chances of her winning her very first time competing at Nationals was unlikely—she'd be up against considerably more experienced riders. But he didn't tell her that. She deserved to dream big. He had once, when he'd first competed. And for a while he'd seen those dreams materialize.

What had *really* happened to him? Brought him to the place he was today, miles below where he'd started? Had Ronnie taken his drive with her when she left, or had Nate thrown it away?

He wasn't a quitter. At least, he hadn't been. He'd fought for his championship wins and climbed the ranks by paying his dues. Then, all of a sudden, he'd let everything that mattered to him go, starting with Ronnie and his career.

Why? Had he allowed her lack of faith in their relationship to make him lose faith in himself? Were all the other excuses—his injury, his best friend moving—just that? Excuses?

Nate's head started to hurt. He couldn't help wondering what Ronnie would she say when she learned Reese was replacing him with a full-time nurse and that rodeo event profits were likely to grow at a snail's pace. Would she send him packing? He'd had a lot to offer her in those long-ago days. An enviable career. Plenty of opportunities. A good income.

He had nothing to offer her now while she, on the other hand, was on her way up. That was hard for him to take, especially after once having such a successful career.

"Sam." He reached an arm through the fence railings and patted Big John's nose. "You have more than enough talent to win. You don't need me. But you need Ronnie, she's the best teacher and trainer around. You also need your parents and younger brothers, because no one loves you more than them. And you need the Hartmans. You haven't known them long, but they're also family and want what's best for you."

Sam made a grumpy face. "My parents haven't seen Ray since I was a baby and they sure haven't met my sisters."

"I'd say rooting for you at Nationals is a good place for them to get acquainted."

"Maybe you're right."

"Happens every once in a while."

"Thanks, Nate." She smiled. "I'm really glad you're here. I hope you stay."

"We'll see." He gave Big John another pat. "Why don't you take this fellow on another spin around the arena and let me get a good look at that leg in motion."

While Sam did as he instructed, Ronnie finished with her call and came over to where he stood. Her expression radiated pure joy. At first, Nate thought he might be the reason, especially when she gave him a big hug.

He was wrong, however. Her excitement had nothing to do with him or them.

"I have news!" she exclaimed. "That was the president of the East Valley Can Chasers. They're a club of junior rodeo barrel racers from Scottsdale. They want to hire me and are willing to pay good money. I mean, *good* money, Nate." She hugged him again. "This is the opportunity I've been waiting for. With the Can Chasers, my school is really going to take off."

Nate summoned a happy smile for her. It wasn't easy. On the inside, he felt hollow and empty.

Chapter Twelve

Ronnie was aware she babbled too fast to be fully understood. She couldn't help herself, she was so excited. Nate asked her more than once to repeat herself, and Ronnie forced a calming breath into her lungs.

"The Can Chasers want me to give lessons one night a week at a private rodeo arena they use in north Scottsdale. From six to nine. And to give Saturday clinics every three months. If I can attend any rodeos with them, they'll pay me extra for that."

"What about the Poco Dinero barrel racing? Won't this interfere?"

"No, not at all," she assured him.

"But you said the Can Chasers want you to attend rodeos and give clinics."

"It won't be a conflict. Not at first." She waved away his concerns, though they were somewhat valid. "We'll iron out all the details on Wednesday. That's when I'm meeting with the president of the club and some of the parents." She let out an exuberant laugh. "I might have to hire an attorney. They're requiring me to sign a one-year contract. That's a little intimidating in case things don't go as expected. Good, though, because I'll have guaranteed income. Did I tell you they're willing to pay a lot?"

"What about Nationals?" Sam asked, leaning forward over Big John's neck, a disgruntled frown on her face. "We're leaving Wednesday."

"The meeting's in the morning."

"You said we needed to be on the road no later than nine."

"Relax, Sam. We'll make up the time along the way."

The teenager's frown turned sad. "Nate's not going with us. He says he has to work."

"Okay." Ronnie would have liked for Nate to accompany them but understood his reasons for remaining behind. In fact, she had enlisted his help in overseeing the barrel racing Saturday afternoon. "It happens. Work's important."

"So's Nationals."

"There's always next year," Nate said.

Ronnie's gaze went from one to the other. They were both considerably underwhelmed by her big news. Granted, it wasn't life changing, but a contract with the Can Chasers would make the difference between Ronnie keeping her rental house and having to find a roommate. Or, worse, having to move back home with her dad and Dolores.

More importantly, the potential to grow her fledgling business was tremendous. The Can Chasers' reputation for excellence extended throughout the entire southwest. As someone associated with the organization, her reputation would benefit.

Instead of cheering her accomplishment, however, Sam pouted and Nate looked like his truck had been repossessed. All because they were leaving a little later for Vegas and he couldn't go with them.

Irritation crept in, tarnishing Ronnie's jubilant mood—which wasn't right. She was entitled to be elated, and, dammit, they should be elated for her.

"Sam," Ronnie said, sounding more sour than she'd intended, "why don't you return Big John to the stables and saddle Comanche. We can start practicing. We have a lot to accomplish today and tomorrow."

No sooner had Sam ridden off than Ronnie turned to Nate. "What's wrong with you two? Aren't you happy for me?"

"Of course we are."

"If that's acting happy, I'd hate to see you when you're miserable."

"Come on, sweetheart. Let's sit. You can tell me all the details."

Nate took her by the arm and walked her to his truck, which he'd parked with the tail end facing the arena. He lowered the gate and hopped on, then sat with his legs swinging and patted the spot beside him. Ronnie settled in next to him, marginally mollified.

"I also have a potential buyer for Comanche. After Nationals, of course. I wouldn't expect Sam to switch to a new horse this late in the game. And I met several people interested in either horse training or barrel racing lessons."

"Besides the Can Chasers?" Nate asked.

She beamed. "These are contacts from both days at the Poco Dinero. It's been a good weekend for me."

"Congratulations." An odd note had crept into his voice.

"I meant to tell you all this last night. Not the part about the Can Chasers, they just called. The rest of it. Only I, we, got sidetracked."

She leaned her shoulder into his, the playful gesture affectionate and comfortable and a reminder of the old days. With so many wonderful things happening to her, she was feeling more than ready to move forward with Nate and take their relationship public. No one would be surprised. Certainly not her family—they'd be ecstatic.

"Right," Nate muttered.

She drew back to study him, utterly baffled by his glaring lack of emotion or enthusiasm.

"Nate, what's wrong? Did something happen between now and this morning? Unless I'm mistaken, you seemed pretty insistent that we see each other." The unthinkable occurred to her. "Have you changed your mind? Do you regret last night? Because I don't. I realize I might have come across as overly cautious. But we talked it through. We agree to go slow. And with me landing all this new business, it feels like things are falling into place for us."

"Reese fired me this morning," he said softly.

"What? Why? I don't believe it. Fired you?"

"Technically, she let me go. She's going to hire a full-time nurse for Theo. In light of his fall yesterday, she's convinced he needs someone with medical training."

"He'll hate that."

"Probably."

"What did he say?"

"I don't know. She hadn't told him yet and asked me not to say anything. I assured her I'd stay through the transition. She's calling in-home nursing services tomorrow."

Ronnie pressed her hands to her cheeks. "Where are you going to go? Did she say you have to move?"

"I assuming I do. Our original deal was me helping with Theo in exchange for rent and board. And to answer your first question, I don't know where I'll go. That will depend on my job situation."

The solution seemed obvious to Ronnie. "Move in with me."

"Not this soon. We agree to go slow."

"Okay, stay in your trailer. Park it out back by the stalls and paddock. My setup isn't that different from

Frankie's. You can hook up to the water and electric, and there's plenty of room for Breeze. It'll cost you nothing."

"I don't take charity," he said firmly.

"Then pay me rent. Or, better yet, come work for me. You're great with Sam. I'm sure you'll be just as good with my other students. And with more horses to train—"

"No."

His brusque response confused her. "Why?"

"There's no way I'm going to work for you."

"I see." She sat up straighter. "Because working for your girlfriend is demoralizing and beneath you."

"That's not the reason."

She didn't believe him. "You need to swallow your pride, Nate."

"If I had any pride, I wouldn't be living in a trailer."

"You lost your job through no fault of your own. Let me help. You can pay me back later."

"I don't want us to start out with me being indebted to you. That'll grow old fast, and you'll start resenting me."

"Ask Dad or Theo for a job." Another good suggestion, in Ronnie's opinion. "I'm sure they'd give you one."

"The Small Change isn't hiring. I overheard Theo and Enrico talking the other day."

"They'll find a job for you."

He shook his head. "Apparently I do have a shred of pride left. I won't take a job manufactured for me because I'm dating the foreman's daughter."

"You're being stubborn."

"I'm not opposed to acting on leads. If your dad or Theo know of anyone hiring, I'll definitely follow up."

She thought he was splitting hairs but didn't argue.

"In the meantime, I'll extend my search outside Mustang Valley to Rio Verde and Casa Grande." He adjusted his cowboy hat, pushing down on the crown. "Maybe the west valley."

"Casa Grande and the west valley? You can't commute that far. You'd have to quit the Poco Dinero."

"I'm hoping to find something that allows me to continue working for Bess on weekends."

"Meaning, we'd only see each other two days a week?" Hardly a promising start for their budding relationship.

"If it comes to that."

"We just got back together and now you want to leave."

"I need a job, Ronnie."

"You could have one. With me or at The Small Change." God, she sounded like a petulant child.

"I gave you my reasons. I was hoping you'd respect them."

"I do respect them."

At what point had their discussion taken such a wrong turn? They should be celebrating her good fortune, not contemplating the possibility of Nate leaving.

"I don't get it," she said. "I'm offering you a place to stay and paying work. I wouldn't be supporting you, I'd be *helping* you. It's what people who care about each other do. If the situation was reversed, you'd do the same for me."

"I'd be taking advantage of you," he insisted. "You weren't considering hiring anyone until I told you I'd lost my job with Theo."

"Doesn't make it a bad idea."

"If you and I move ahead in this relationship, it's important to me that I contribute my share."

"If?" She resisted the urge to pull away and instead hear him out.

"When you and I were together, I had a lot to offer. Now, I have next to nothing."

A very unpleasant thought struck her. "Do you blame me for that?"

He stared at her in disbelief and shock. "Why would you think such a thing?"

"Because me walking out on you was what sent you into a—what did you call it? A tailspin."

"How I handled you walking out was my decision, and I didn't make the best ones. That was hardly your fault."

By now, Sam had emerged from the stables riding Comanche. They entered the arena, joining the other barrel racers there to practice. She didn't appear to notice the tension escalating between Ronnie and Nate as she trotted past them.

"I went out on an emotional limb for you," Ronnie said when Sam was beyond earshot. "Trust me, that wasn't easy. And what happens? You reject me."

"I'm not sure why you're upset," he said. "I'm thinking me finding work out of town fits right in with our plans to go slow."

"What I'm hearing is you're leaving—which *has* been your track record of late—and trying to let me down easy." She was baiting him but unable to stop herself. He *was* rejecting her, whether he admitted it or not.

"Wow, that was below the belt."

"It's as if you don't care enough about me to fight for us."

From his startled look, she might have slapped him. "That's the same way I felt when I came home to find you and all your stuff gone. I thought you didn't care enough about me and our future to stay and fight."

"You didn't come after me."

"What were you doing?" His tone was one of incredulity. "Putting me through some kind of test?"

She swallowed a groan. "Not a test. That was the wrong thing to say."

"You told me yourself, you didn't answer my calls and texts because you were afraid you'd weaken and say yes if I asked you come back."

"That was true. For a while. But then I kept hearing all the things your mom said to me in the hospital and started questioning myself. Before long, I believed not only was I responsible for the miscarriage and unfit to be a mother, I was also undeserving of your love." To Ronnie's dismay, she choked on the last sentence.

"You couldn't be more wrong."

"Feelings and emotions aren't always logical. That doesn't change the impact they can have on our decisions and our lives."

They were both silent for several moments before Nate asked, "Did we rush things?"

"I think we did. We had a lot of issues that were never resolved."

Tears stung her eyes as a wave of loss and despair consumed her. They hadn't been back together a full day, and already they were on the verge of breaking up.

"Not entirely." He exhaled a long breath. "I want to be ready for a commitment with you. I'm just not sure I am."

"You seemed sure this morning."

"My outlook has changed." His demeanor had gone from angry to defeated. "Having the rug pulled out from under you does that."

"You aren't giving us a chance," Ronnie protested, very much aware their roles were reversed from six years ago. Then, she'd been the one eager to flee, and he'd been the one fighting to stay together.

"You deserve more than a guy with a part-time job and an old horse and who lives in his trailer."

"You have much more to offer me than that," she insisted.

"It's taken all this time, but I finally understand why you turned down my proposal. You weren't in a good place then to make a commitment, and I'm not now." He took her limp hand in his and rubbed the knuckles with the pad of his thumb. "What if we…gave each other some space while I look for a job and you focus on your business? Neither of us needs any added pressure right now."

"Are you sure you don't mean permanent space?" The question tore from her throat.

"I don't want to hurt you, Ronnie."

She peered at him through her tears. "That isn't an answer."

"Try to understand. Until I'm happy with the person I am and the direction of my life, I can't make you happy."

That was almost word for word what Ronnie had told herself when she was leaving Nate.

"What if Reese hadn't let you go?" she asked. "Would we be having this conversation?"

"I think so. If not today, eventually."

Removing her hand from his, she pushed off the tailgate and landed on her feet. "I'd better help Sam with practice."

"Are you going to be okay?" Pain filled his eyes.

"Of course. We were together for one day, Nate. Not even one day. Let's call it a fling to get each other out of our systems."

She walked away then, fully aware there was no getting him out of her system. She'd tried before, and failed. After the past few weeks, it would only be harder.

NATE REACHED HIS hand across the table he shared with Spence Bohanan at the Poco Dinero. "Can't tell you how much I appreciate this."

Spence returned the firm shake. "Glad I could help."

Nate motioned for the waitress to bring their lunch tab. When Spence offered to pay, Nate insisted, "I've got this."

Spence's buddy owned a racing quarter horse farm in Florence, about an hour or so from Mustang Valley. The man was looking to hire a stable manager. Not exactly Nate's line of work, but as a favor to Spence, he'd agreed to interview Nate.

"You'll like him," Spence continued. "He's a straight shooter."

"Just glad he's willing to consider me. Reese hired full-time nursing help for Theo, starting tomorrow."

"Call me if you need a place to park your trailer for a couple days."

"I hate to impose."

"You're practically family."

"That's a stretch."

"I disagree," Spence said. "Without your help, Sam wouldn't have qualified for Nationals."

"Ronnie deserves all the credit. It's a shame Sam didn't make it past the first round."

"Does anyone their first time there?"

"Not often."

Sam and Ronnie had arrived home last week. While Sam had started out well in Vegas, she was outperformed by older and more experienced competitors. As a result, the teenager was more determined than ever to qualify again this coming year on Big John. Everyone agreed the horse would be competition ready by February. March at the latest.

Spence set down his empty beer bottle. "Look, it's none of my business, but Ronnie's taking whatever happened between the two of you pretty hard."

"Yeah?" Nate tried to hide his interest. "What did she say?"

"You know Ronnie. It's what she doesn't say."

He doubted she'd told Spence and the rest of the Hartmans about what had transpired between them. Likely, they were making educated guesses. But it was true that when Ronnie felt bad she clammed up.

According to Sam, Ronnie was busy working long hours with her clients, new and old, and the East Valley Can Chasers. Nate was glad; she deserved the success coming to her.

"Probably just as well I'll be relocating." And he would be, one way or the other. If not this job, he'd find another one.

Spence reached for his jacket. "Florence isn't that far. And aren't you staying on here as bull riding manager?"

"If possible. Just depends."

A stable manager's schedule could be hectic. Long and late hours if one of the horses was sick or injured.

"You can't avoid Ronnie forever," Spence said.

"I'm not trying."

"The hell you aren't."

Nate and Ronnie had crossed paths only once during the past eight days. It happened when he'd visited Sam the day after her return from Nationals. Running into each other at Frankie's had been a surprise and after recovering their composure, they'd been civil. Even cordial.

He'd wanted to talk, but it wasn't the time or place for a private conversation. Besides, Ronnie had thrown up all sorts of invisible barricades. What else was new?

Well, she was understandably hurt. As she'd said the other day when they had their argument, she put herself out there only to have him reject her. Nate knew better than anyone how that felt.

Did she realize she'd done the same thing to him? He was curious but not enough to ask.

He missed her more than he'd thought possible and, despite everything, had almost pulled her aside at Frankie's to tell her he'd reconsidered. The next moment, he'd come to his senses. Nothing had changed, and they were no more ready for or capable of a lasting relationship than they had been before he'd lost his job as Theo's caregiver.

That didn't stop Nate from feeling the break anew. Each day it was a struggle for him to rise and put on a smiling face. This time, however, instead of loading his truck and trailer and heading for parts unknown, he was determined to stay—at least until he found a new job— and battle the dark cloud hanging over him.

What would have happened if he'd accepted Ronnie's offer to stay with her? Granted, he did have his pride, but he wasn't someone who believed in double standards. Both partners in a relationship were equal, deciding together on their personal definition of equal. Ronnie felt similarly, which was one of the reasons winning a title had been so important to her. She'd wanted to bring that accomplishment into their relationship.

Had her desire to be on equal footing with him been the reason she'd competed at Nationals when he'd asked her not to? He hadn't blamed her for the miscarriage, but neither had he assumed any responsibility. Maybe he should have, for putting unrealistic expectations on her.

"Call me after the interview," Spence said, standing up and donning his jacket.

"I will."

Nate didn't leave with Spence. Rather, he went to find Bess. He'd informed his boss he was looking for a job, assuring her he wouldn't leave her in a bind. They'd discussed various courses of action should Nate be unable to continue as bull riding manager.

The second weekend of rodeo events had drawn about the same number of people as the first, which was encouraging. The locals who hadn't returned for a second time were replaced by out-of-towners traveling greater distances.

It was too early to predict whether future attendance would increase or decrease. Bess remained the queen of optimism, claiming the Poco Dinero was the only place in five hundred miles offering both recreational bull riding *and* barrel racing. If she added bull riding lessons, the saloon would be one of a kind.

"Why so glum?" she asked when Nate leaned an elbow on the bar. Business was slow—the lunch crowd had left, and the happy hour crowd wouldn't trickle in for a while yet.

"Do I look glum?" So much for fooling everyone.

Shutting off the water at the small stainless-steel sink, she tossed a dish towel over her bony shoulder. "I've seen dogs on their way to the pound acting happier."

"I have a lot on my mind." Nate proceeded to fill her in on the interview.

"Sounds like a great opportunity. He's including board for you and your horse. Can't beat that. And Spence wouldn't steer you wrong."

"The guy hasn't offered me the job, and I haven't taken it."

"We'll see." Her tone implied him accepting was a given.

"If he doesn't agree to me having Friday evenings and Saturdays off, at least until you hire my replacement, I won't take the job."

"Course you will, if it's the right one for you. Don't decide until you've talked to him."

Nate leaned in and gave her a sound peck on the cheek. "You're a special lady, you know that?"

"Oh, for pity's sake." She pretended to be annoyed and pushed at him. "Get away from me."

Nate's next stop was The Small Change to visit Theo. As expected, the older man had been furious with Reese, but had taken his fury out on Nate. Today was no different, and telling Theo about the interview only worsened his mood.

"You're abandoning me!" Theo roared from his favorite place at the living room wet bar.

"I don't want to go, trust me."

"I'm firing that nurse the moment she arrives tomorrow."

Nate couldn't help smiling, appreciating Theo's loyalty to him. "Reese is only doing what she thinks is best. She's at the bank all day. Your son-in-law runs the ranch. And sooner or later, they're going to start a family."

"Why can't you be here every day?"

"I have no medical trailing. I'm not even an accredited caregiver."

"Florence!" Theo bit out the town's name as if it left a bad taste in his mouth. "A racing quarter horse farm. What's wrong with working for me?"

"You have more than enough hands already."

"You're leaving just because you and Ray's daughter got into a spat."

Nate had told Theo a little about the situation with Ronnie. He'd probably heard more from Ronnie's dad. "It wasn't just a spat."

"Do you love her?"

"I..." Nate paused, weighing his answer. He'd loved

her more than life itself six years ago. What about now? "Yes," he admitted, "and I probably always will."

"Then stay and fight for her, by golly." Theo smacked the bar top, almost unseating himself. "Quit running off every time you hit a little bump."

"I'm not running off. I'm seizing my next adventure. That's what Allan always said to do."

"Bullshit. What your brother meant was for you to live your life to the fullest, whatever that turns out to be. Not turn your back on family and friends. There's a difference."

Nate recalled the many conversations he'd had with his brother, especially those near then end when Allan was practically an invalid. He had desperately longed for the one thing he could never have—freedom. The ability to go where he chose and do what he chose. Completely unencumbered.

Theo was right. Nate had been making excuses, and Allan wouldn't have approved. Worse, he'd be disappointed in Nate.

"If I'd understood that two decades ago—" Theo's gaze turned inward "—my wife might not have left me for another man. Instead of appreciating what was right under my nose, I was always chasing something I really didn't need."

"You make an interesting point," Nate said.

Theo snorted. "I make a *damn good* point."

"You're kind of smart for an old guy with Parkinson's."

"Tell you what." He pointed a finger at Nate. "You answer my questions honestly, and I'll support whatever you decide. Stay, go, work in Florence or for me."

Nate didn't need Theo's support or approval. Then again, what harm would it do to play along with him? "Sure. Fire away."

"Of all the jobs you've had, which one gave you the most satisfaction?"

Nate didn't hesitate. "Taking care of my brother. Don't get me wrong, it was hard most days. Allan could be difficult. But I never minded because in a small way, I made a difference."

Theo gave a satisfied nod. "And of all the places you've lived, which one made you the happiest?"

"I like San Antonio." Nate chuckled. "But if I were to pick one—"

"Mustang Valley. Right. Next question."

"Wait, you didn't let me answer."

Theo's brows shot up. "Do I need to?"

"Hmm. Maybe not," Nate relented.

"And I don't need to ask who you've loved most in the world. We already covered that."

"Why am I even doing this?"

"So, here's my last question and don't answer right away. Think on it for a minute. If time and money weren't factors, what would you do? No limitations."

Nate did think on it and when he answered, he surprised himself with his honesty. "I'd go to college and get a degree."

"In what?"

"Nursing or physical therapy. I think I'd be good at either. Allan always said I had a knack for nurturing, which sounds kind of funny for a bull rider, I guess."

Theo broke into a wide, delighted grin. "Well, hot damn. What's stopping you?"

"Time and money. Well, money anyway. I'm broke."

"Where there's a will, there's a way."

"Mr. McGraw, sir—"

"Just listen." He then made a proposition that Nate found daunting and also intriguing. "What do you think?"

"Honestly, I have a hundred reasons to say no."

"And three really good ones to say yes."

Nate tried convincing himself Theo was a crazy old man. Go to college? Who was he kidding? Nate hadn't cracked a book in years. And to be so beholden to one person? What if he failed?

Then again, what if he didn't? He'd probably never get an opportunity like this again.

Crossing the five feet separating him and Theo, he pulled the older man into a bear hug. "Sir, you have deal."

Chapter Thirteen

"Take him around once more," Ronnie shouted to Sam and motioned with her hand.

The teenager was riding Teddy Bear, a three-year-old exquisitely marked palomino with the gentle personality of his namesake. Also, and this part worried Ronnie, the same amount of brains as a stuffed toy. He was slow to catch on and quick to forget.

His owners were new clients—she'd met them during that first weekend at the Poco Dinero. There was no question Teddy Bear had looks and, when he wanted, speed. What he may not have was a career in professional barrel racing.

With luck and a little maturity, he might improve. Ronnie had been surprised before. Besides, Teddy Bear's owners were paying her handsomely to give her best effort and the horse a chance. Their daughter absolutely adored "Bear-Bear" and was determined to eventually compete on him.

When Sam completed her circuit of the arena, Ronnie instructed her to cool down Teddy Bear and return him to his stall.

"Okay, but then can I ride Big John?" She'd been assisting Ronnie all day with the promise that Ronnie would assess Big John's recent progress.

"All right. Just don't rush. Teddy Bear worked up a sweat."

Sam laughed. "You're such a mother hen."

Ronnie had to admit, her younger sister's often unpredictable demeanor was significantly improved of late. She'd expected Sam to return from Nationals with a permanent scowl, a refusal to cooperate and total dissatisfaction with everyone and everything.

Instead, Sam had immediately buckled down, showing a willingness to do whatever was necessary to resume competing in February. A 2.0 version of herself.

Other than Sam not advancing, Nationals had gone well. Their father and Dolores had flown in for two days. Joining them had been Sam's mother, adoptive father and two younger brothers. The meeting could have been awkward but wasn't. Everyone was there to support Sam, and they'd let that guide their behavior. No one dredged up the past or cast blame or even mentioned the string of lies that had originally brought Sam to Mustang Valley in search of her biological father.

As a result, Ronnie was able to say she found Sam's "other family" to be genuinely nice and eagerly anticipated seeing them again in the near future, when they came to visit Sam. Ronnie was also impressed by her father's readiness to extend the hand of friendship. She suspected he and Sam had grown closer as a result, though her adoptive father would always be her dad—the man who had raised her and loved her as his own.

While Sam's parents still weren't thrilled with her decision to forgo college and pursue a professional rodeo career, they were willing to respect her wishes. At one point, Ronnie overheard Sam's parents offering to pay for a portion of her expenses. Ronnie considered that a huge step forward, and was pleased for Sam. She knew how expensive the sport of rodeo could be, particularly in the beginning.

At that moment, another of her students made an appearance, bringing her back to the present. With local schools on winter break this week and next for the holidays, Ronnie's schedule was bursting at the seams. She was teaching a group lesson this afternoon and a private one after that.

No sooner had she told the student to warm up her horse in the arena than her phone rang. Recognizing the president of the Can Chasers' number—they'd been talking frequently since their meeting—Ronnie answered right away and spent the next five minutes finalizing the remaining details of their contract.

So far, Ronnie loved the Can Chasers. They were a top-notch, serious-minded organization with outstanding work ethics. Plus, the young women were a delight, their enthusiasm catching and their dedication admirable. Not least of all, the private rodeo arena they used was well-maintained and boasted every piece of equipment a barrel racing instructor could ask for.

Ronnie predicted a long and mutually beneficial relationship with them, along with the new clients she'd recently added to her roster. Also encouraging, the sign-ups for this coming weekend's barrel racing event were already ahead of last week's, much to Bess's delight.

Why then, Ronnie asked herself, wasn't she over the moon with happiness, walking on sunshine and every other lame cliché ever written?

Her business was growing, her family was happy, healthy and thriving, and, thanks to an increase in income, she was able to continue living in the house she loved.

But instead of feeling happy, she had to power through her days and remember to smile whenever anyone glanced in her direction.

This couldn't all be because of Nate, could it? One night together didn't automatically mean they'd resumed their relationship, so they couldn't have broken up, right? They never even went on that date Nate had talked about.

She sighed, half with longing and half with regret. It *had* been an incredible night—which he'd blown the next day by announcing he was leaving.

All right, not leaving. She'd made that leap and possibly pushed him into a decision when he'd only wanted some leeway to find a new job. But she'd been mad, dammit, and—in her opinion—justifiably mad. He could have moved in with her and helped with her business. She hadn't been offering him a handout, regardless of how he'd interpreted it. Had anyone else made him the offer, he'd have taken it on the spot.

In hindsight, she conceded she could have expressed herself more articulately. Not let her anger get the better of her and shut down completely when he didn't immediately side with her.

She'd done that before, years ago, which had ended with her walking out. Now, Nate was the one walking out on her.

A miscommunication, misunderstanding, misstep, call it what you will. She and Nate had had too many to count—including her decision to compete when she was pregnant and her rejection of his proposal. And now this last one. She should have proclaimed she'd stand by him no matter what, even if she didn't like his decision.

Wasn't that what Sam's parents had done, agreed to support her unconditionally regardless of their objections? And Ronnie had witnessed the positive effect it had had on Sam's mood and outlook.

Too bad she hadn't given Nate the same consideration. He might be here now rather than…where?

Last she'd heard from her father, Reese had retained

a nursing service for Theo. She'd offered to let Nate continue staying at the ranch, but he'd refused. Ronnie knew how important it was for him to pay his own way. Hadn't they argued at length about that very thing? Maybe Bess would let him park his trailer behind the rodeo arena if push came to shove. And surely he could leave Breeze at The Small Change a while longer. What was one more horse among the thirty or forty head Theo already owned?

Ronnie would impose on her father if it came to that, though she probably wouldn't find out what happened to Nate, not immediately and not from him.

A fresh pang of sadness struck. She resisted the tears threatening to spill, as she'd been doing all week. For someone used to keeping her emotions in check, she was having the worst time lately.

Why couldn't she go to him? Apologize and ask for a second chance?

Fear of rejection?

Fear he'd say yes?

Not for the first time Ronnie wondered if she was terrified of failing and had competed at Nationals when Nate pleaded with her not to rather than divulge her deep, dark secret.

Looking back, she knew her heart hadn't been in competing that last year. Perhaps she'd suffered from burnout or changing interests, a lack of confidence brought on by her inability to win a title or any number of other reasons.

She hadn't confided in Nate, convinced his opinion of her would change, and they'd drift apart. Rodeo was the only thing they'd had in common. At least, that was what she'd thought. Ronnie had abandoned him before giving them a chance to discover what else they loved about each other and to build an even stronger relationship.

At home, she'd used the miscarriage as an excuse to quit rodeoing, refusing to admit to her waning interest in competing that had started long before then.

She couldn't help thinking about how different both her and Nate's lives might have turned out if she'd only been honest with him. And honest with herself.

Ronnie wrapped her arms around her middle. Self-examination was a difficult and uncomfortable process, and she tried to push away the unwanted thoughts. They refused and insisted on further scrutiny. It was akin to banging herself in the head with a hammer, and Ronnie's chin fell under the onslaught.

Sam rode up on Big John, giving Ronnie a start. How long had she been standing there, staring into space?

"What do you think?" Sam asked, pulling the horse to a stop in front of Ronnie. "He's not limping one bit."

"No? Good." Ronnie didn't want to admit she hadn't been watching.

The teenager dismounted, and together they examined the horse's leg. Ronnie admitted the residual swelling appeared to have completely subsided.

"What's wrong with you?" Sam abruptly straightened and stared at Ronnie.

"Nothing." She dropped Big John's foot.

"You've been weird all day. You've been weird since before we left for Nationals."

"I don't know what you're talking about," Ronnie lied through her teeth.

"Is it Nate?"

"What? No."

"He has a job interview in Florence."

The name of the town rang a bell with Ronnie. "Spence has a friend in Florence who owns a racing quarter horse farm."

"Well, that's where Nate has the interview."

"You saw him?"

"He called."

"Oh."

"He doesn't want to go." Sam ignored Big John, who pawed the ground, impatient to return to his workout.

Ronnie was reluctant to ask but did anyway. "What makes you say that?"

"He likes it here. He likes you." Sam planted her hands on her hips. "And you like him. Except you're both too pigheaded to admit it."

"Things are complicated, Sam."

"Uncomplicate them."

"Not that easy."

"It's as hard or simple as you make it, Ronnie. Take it from me."

The sage wisdom of an eighteen-year-old.

"I messed up bad when I found out Ray was my biological father and my parents hid that from me my entire life."

"It was a lot to deal with."

"Yeah, but I made things worse by copping an attitude. You told me that enough times. Luckily, when I finally did listen, it wasn't too late. Now look at me. I have two families. I almost didn't have any."

Ronnie went still, the words Sam said sinking in. It was one thing for Ronnie to realize how badly she'd screwed up with Nate, it was another for others to notice.

Maybe she shouldn't have rejected Nate's long-ago Valentine's Day proposal and, instead, asked for the necessary time to recover from their loss. Later, when they were both ready, they could have considered marriage. They'd been young, after all, with no reason to rush.

Except Ronnie had been too wrapped up in herself, her grief and her guilt to see a clear path and had panicked.

Funny how alike she and Nate were. He'd been dealt a blow when Reese let him go and had panicked, assuming the answer was to hit the road. Old habits were hard to break, especially when the person who supposedly cared withheld their support.

"You should talk to him." Sam moved close and put an arm around Ronnie's shoulders. It was almost as if she were the older sister and Ronnie the younger one.

"I think it might be too late." Her voice cracked slightly.

"Maybe not." Sam gave her another squeeze. "Why else would he be here now?"

Ronnie spun to see Nate's truck pulling into the ranch. "What in the world…?"

"My guess is he wants to see you. He sure didn't come all this way to see me."

Breathe, Ronnie told herself. *Focus*.

"Hi, Nate!" Sam waved wildly when he emerged from his parked truck.

Ronnie squeezed her eyes shut. What was wrong with him? He seemed to be walking in slow motion. After an eternity passed, he came to stand in front of her.

"Hi, Ronnie. Sam."

"I've got to exercise Big John before the lesson starts." Sam gave him a quick hug. "See you later." She hesitated. "I *will* see you later?"

"Probably. We'll see."

"Whoo-hoo!" She hopped on Big John and trotted off.

Ronnie had yet to speak. She couldn't; her jaw hung loosely, unwilling to cooperate.

"You have a few minutes?" Nate asked. "To talk?"

She knew in that instant how she answered him would

dictate their entire future. Yes, they'd have one. No, he'd turn around and disappear from her life forever.

Hoping and praying she was making the right choice, she met his gaze and nodded.

NATE COULDN'T HELP thinking how similar this scene was to his first day in Mustang Valley. Like then, he'd arrived at Powell Ranch to find Ronnie and Sam together examining Big John. Ronnie wore her Arizona Cardinals hoodie and her long blond hair fell in a braid down her back just like before.

The sight of her sent a powerful zing through him straight to the center of his heart. He'd had the same reaction at the New Mexico State Fair Rodeo so long ago when he'd watched a startling young beauty blaze into the arena on the fastest horse there, a look of sheer determination on her face. He'd been smitten with her then and still was, regardless of, or maybe because of, everything they'd been through.

There were a lot of differences between the day he'd arrived and now, he couldn't help noting. Ronnie and Sam weren't at odds, and Big John was almost fully recovered. Sam had reached her dream of going to Nationals and resolved her differences with her family.

Perhaps the biggest changes were to Nate himself. Instead of wandering aimlessly, he'd found a purpose ripe with promise and rich with potential. He was gainfully employed and likely to stay employed. No more temporary side jobs for him.

All that remained was Ronnie. She was the last missing piece in the completion of his plan.

Wait a minute. Plan? She was infinitely more to him than that. More than his first love and his one true love. Ronnie was air and food and sunshine. She was the guardian of his heart, the shelter he sought and the best reason to better himself.

If he could convince her of all these things, that he'd been an idiot not to realize it sooner, they might have a fighting chance.

"Did you come to tell me goodbye?" she asked. "I heard from Sam you have a job interview in Florence."

"Had an interview," he corrected her.

Confusion marred her features. "I don't understand."

Nate glanced around, seeking a less public location. The discussion he hoped to have with her didn't need an audience. Not that people were staring. They were, however, casting plenty of interested glances. Sam in particular.

"Come on," he said and captured her hand when she didn't immediately respond.

"Where are you taking me?"

"For a short walk." There'd be fewer people on the other side of the horse stables.

She didn't move. "What's going on, Nate?"

"I called and canceled my interview with Spence's friend in Florence."

"Why?"

"I'm staying on at The Small Change." This time, when he tugged on her hand, she followed him.

"I thought Reese hired a nursing service."

"She did. Eight hours a day, five days a week. I'll cover for the nurse the other two days, Wednesdays and Saturdays. Theo insisted. I'll be driving him to his monthly Cattlemen's Association meetings and his poker games, the rodeo events at the Poco Dinero, the Phoenix Suns' games when he has tickets, and anywhere else he wants to go without a nurse tagging along. I'll also get him up, showered and dressed every morning and stay with him every evening when I'm not working for Bess."

"Really? Okay." Her tone was skeptical. "How is that different from before, if I can ask?"

"On the surface, not much, other than I'll be working a lot more hours. Plus, I agreed to be on call to help whenever I'm needed. Reese and Theo were able to compromise, once she calmed down. He'd agree to the nurse on the condition I was allowed to stay on and that I get paid. But in addition to wages, Theo's funding my college expenses."

"College?" Ronnie's confusion increased. "I don't understand."

They fell into an easy stroll very reminiscent of what Nate had envisioned when he'd suggested a date. "I'm registering at Scottsdale Community College. Nursing classes. I'll start after winter break."

He expected her to accuse him of joking or ask him where he got such a ridiculous notion. She didn't. Taking him by complete surprise, she showed him all over again why she was the only woman for him.

"That's wonderful! I'm so happy for you."

She stopped and hugged him briefly. He wanted to hold her forever, along the lines of till death do us part, but he was getting ahead of himself.

"Thanks. I'm actually pretty excited."

"You'll be great," she continued. "I know how rewarding it was for you to help with Allan's care."

His chest tightened, his emotions expanding and struggling to find room in the confined space. "Yeah, it was."

"He'd be proud of you."

Nate marveled at her compassion. She alone understood how close he'd been to his late brother and the depths of their bond. "He'd kick me in the rear end for taking this long to figure out what I wanted to do."

"Are you going to keep working at the Poco Dinero?"

"Absolutely. I'm not giving that up." The job with Theo would only provide pocket change.

"Because you can't let Bess down?"

"Because it seems quitting bull riding is impossible for me no matter how hard I try. Not that I'm competing anymore. But I didn't realize how much I missed the action and excitement until Bess hired me."

"Trust me, I can relate. I love teaching barrel racing and training horses for those very same reasons."

"It's obvious. And you're great at what you do."

Her bright smile restored and revitalized him. How different things might have turned out if he'd refused his mother's request to stop in Mustang Valley on his way to Houston.

"Thank goodness you're not competing anymore," Ronnie said. "I hate to admit it, but I couldn't handle you getting injured. You came too close the other night, and you weren't even on a bull."

"I like having you worry about me."

"I doubt I'll ever stop."

Every cell in his being ached to kiss her. He resisted, and it was torture. "Won't be easy, working and going to school. I've been slacking off for a while now."

"You were never afraid of hard work, Nate."

He stared, admiring all the qualities about her that made her so special. She could have refused to talk to him. Could have maintained her distance. Instead, she was open and warm and encouraging. Whatever they'd been through, she was and always would be his friend. Was she ready for more? He couldn't be sure.

"I have you to thank," he said.

"Me? No way. Sounds like you have Theo to thank."

"I suspect he'll run me ragged."

"How? By making you take him to his poker games?"

She laughed, the sound light and joyous and giving Nate hope. Ronnie wasn't throwing up barriers or drawing invisible lines. She wasn't shutting herself off.

"Hey, those chips are heavy."

She groaned.

"Maybe you can help me study."

"Ah!"

They'd reached a critical moment, and Nate sensed she knew it, too. They either quit now and went their separate ways or took a leap. It was completely up to Ronnie.

Gazing straight into his eyes, she asked, "What are you *really* suggesting?"

He surrendered to his longing and reached for her hands. Her skin was like satin, cool but instantly warming to his touch.

"Us having a second chance, only to throw it away, finally penetrated my thick skull. I can't bear the thought of losing the most important person in the world to me. You."

"Believe me, I like hearing that. But I can't forget what you said the other day. Is going to college and working part-time enough for you to feel you're contributing to the relationship?"

"I still won't have two dollars to rub together for a while. A long while, probably. But I can support myself, if not in the lap of luxury. I have a solid direction for my life and a future in a career I'm confident I'll like. That's more than I could say a month ago."

"Very true."

"If you can wait a year or two for this diamond in the

rough to shine, I think you might be happy with the results."

He thought she might jump in his arms as she had before and kiss him soundly, exclaiming, "Yes, yes, yes!" Instead, she simply stood there, and his heart started to sink.

"I wouldn't want for us to wind up in the same place as before," she finally said.

He understood her being cautious. "You're right. We have a lot to overcome." Recognizing her need for assurance, he squeezed her fingers. "I'll say it, I'm not afraid. I love you, Ronnie. I always have and always will. We'll have our ups and downs. Just think how much more we'll value what we have because of how hard we fought for it."

The tiny upward curve of her lips was the first sign, followed by her leaning in closer.

"I love you, too," she whispered so softly he barely heard. "Could the third time be the charm?"

He didn't wait for her to make the first move. Dropping her hands, he lifted her by the waist and held her high in the air. The emotions fighting for room in his chest erupted in a loud, "Yee-haw!"

She laughed again and, when he finally put her down, said, "We go slow. That hasn't changed from before. One day at a time."

"You call the shots, sweetheart." He cradled her cheek with his palm.

"I'd also think we should visit your folks and make peace with your mom. Or, they can come here."

"She'd like the chance to make amends, I'm sure."

"Okay."

"Is that it?"

"Of course not. You know me." She stood on her tiptoes and pressed her lips to his in a sweet, gentle kiss that, as always, was infinitely more electrifying than their passionate ones.

Nate imagined them a few years down the road, the two of them married, living in Ronnie's house—only now as homeowners rather than renters—her running her business and him graduating with a nursing degree. He kept the images to himself. Eventually, when the moment was right, he'd share them with her.

"I do have one request." She flung her arms around his neck. "If you're free, I'd like to take you to the Valentine's Day dinner and dance."

Nate dipped her backward over his arm. "I accept," he said before his mouth claimed hers.

Epilogue

Two months later

"What's he doing?" Frankie shouted in Ronnie's ear in order to be heard above the country band's rowdy music.

"I don't know," Ronnie shouted back, watching Nate as he approached the band and passed something to the steel guitar player.

The two sisters stood at the end of the buffet line that had been set up for the Valentine's Day dance and dinner. Couples had immediately resumed two-stepping to the music even before dinner ended.

Obviously, the food was a huge hit, given that the buffet line looked like a deserted battleground. Beans and coleslaw remnants were stuck to the sides of chafing dishes. Crumbs littered and barbecue stains dotted the once pristine white linen tablecloths. Pieces of broken plasticware were strewn about, and overturned condiment boats spilled what remained of their contents.

"Do you think he made a song request?" Frankie shouted.

"Maybe." Though why Nate would request a song, Ronnie had no clue.

They'd been together every day for the past two months, together every night for the past two weeks. That was when he'd moved in with Ronnie. Her suggestion, not his. And, yes, she'd been the one to insist they proceed slowly, only to change her mind.

What could she say? Asking him had felt right, and

nothing yet had changed her mind. If anything, she was convinced they were going to succeed this time. For good. Life together was that wonderful.

They'd learned from their mistakes and continued to learn more about each other with every passing day. Nate had become a neat freak during the last six years. Who'd have guessed? She, to his shock, had developed the habit of watching the nightly news before going to bed and eating vegan dinners once a week.

Ronnie had finally hired an assistant for her business. After considering several candidates, she'd decided on a former student. The gal was a fireball, and already Ronnie had been able to reduce her sixty-hour workweek to forty-five. More time to spend with Nate.

The recent holidays had flown by in a hectic haze, with Nate's parents coming for a short visit. Nate's mom had been sweet and apologetic and, after muddling through their initial hesitancy, she and Ronnie had gotten along fine. Both his parents repeatedly expressed their delight at Ronnie and Nate's renewed relationship, which gladdened Ronnie and healed the last of her old wounds.

"Look at Sam." Frankie pointed, drawing Ronnie's attention away from Nate and redirecting it to the dance floor where the youngest Hartman sister danced with her boyfriend.

Ronnie chuckled at the sight of him looking utterly out of his element in a cowboy hat and boots. "What won't he do for her?"

"I think they're adorable."

"I think *they're* adorable." She pointed at Mel and Aaron.

The deputy sheriff had his arms as far around his wife's enormous belly as they would go and was guiding her across the dance floor. She wasn't due for another week, though from the size of her she could go into labor at any second.

They were having a boy. The first in the Hartman family for two generations. It was supposed to be a surprise, but Mel had told Ronnie and then made her swear to keep the secret. Except, she'd also told Frankie, and Aaron's daughter Kaylee. Probably the only one who didn't know was Aaron.

Ronnie crossed her fingers the baby would be born by Frankie and Spence's wedding, less than a month away. Mel insisted on inducing labor if two more weeks went by without Aaron junior making an appearance. Ronnie believed her, too.

"Come on." She reached for the nearest chafing dish. "I'll help you clean up."

Frankie patted her on the shoulder. "I accept your kind offer."

At that moment, the song came to an end. Rather than launching into the next one, the steel guitar player stood and removed his microphone from its stand.

"Ladies and gentlemen, cowboys and cowgals, if we can have your attention. My friend here has an announcement to make." The man reached down and delivered the mike to someone in the crowd.

"What's this?" Frankie asked. "Oh, my God. It's Nate."

She was right. The crowd parted as Nate made his way to the center of the hastily emptying dance floor.

Ronnie's heart rate promptly escalated. She had the unmistakable feeling that whatever Nate was doing involved her.

"Ronnie." He started toward her. "Come on out here, sweetheart."

She shook her head, suddenly embarrassed as a hundred gazes all zeroed in on her.

Frankie gave her a push. "Go!"

Caught between her sister and Nate, she had no choice but to take a step forward. From the corner of her eye, she noticed Spence and Dolores holding up their cell phones and taking videos.

"What are you doing?" she whispered when she got close to Nate, tugging nervously on the tail of her braid.

They stood toe to toe, almost nose to nose. Nate's grin lit his entire face. But rather than address her, he spoke into the microphone.

"Ronnie Hartman, six years ago today, I asked you to marry me."

The entire bar went still when Nate's free hand dug into the front pocket of his jeans. Ronnie's breath caught. Her feet seemed to float above the floor and her cheeks burned.

He pulled out a small red velvet box she instantly recognized.

"I know we agreed to take things day by day. And if you tell me no, be warned, I'm going to ask you again. And again and again until you say yes."

In the background, Mel let out a high-pitched gasp. Frankie cheered and someone, possibly Bess, said, "About damn time."

Ronnie stared at the velvet box, noting every detail right down to the jeweler's stamp, the little gold hinges and the slight tremor in Nate's fingers.

When she spoke, her voice came out shaky. "Nate."

He lowered his head and dropped a kiss to the top of hers. Then, using his thumb, he flipped open the box, revealing the same ring he'd proposed with six years ago.

"Will you marry me, Ronnie Hartman, and be my Valentine, today and always?"

The room went completely silent, as if everyone there were holding their breath.

She couldn't take her eyes off the twinkling heart-shaped solitaire nestled in the box. The last time she'd seen the ring, she'd turned down his proposal. And while things were fantastic with them, they weren't quite ready to charge full steam ahead.

"We don't have to set a date," he coaxed. "Just say yes, and we'll figure out the rest later."

Ronnie gazed into the face she'd never stopped loving or longing for. Here was everything she'd ever wanted. Not a championship title but a wonderful man who'd proven beyond any doubt he loved her to distraction and would go the distance for her. For *them*. A man who would be a wonderful father one day when they finally did have a child, and an incredible nurse.

"What's the hold up?" Theo shouted from the bar where he sat on his customary stool. "Put the poor man out of his misery, for crying out loud."

Ronnie sighed. "If I say yes, does he come as part of the deal?"

"'Fraid so." Nate's grin widened, if that was possible. "I couldn't shake him if I tried."

"You're lucky I have a soft spot where he's concerned."

Nate whooped and dropped the mike. Hauling her to him with his free arm, he planted a kiss on her lips as everyone in the Poco Dinero erupted in cheers and applause.

"Wait," Ronnie protested when he finally released her, "I didn't accept."

No one heard her. No one cared. The next instant, Nate took her left hand in his and placed the ring on her finger. She thought she might cry. And then she did. Just for a moment. After that, she was too distracted by family and friends swarming her and Nate.

"Welcome to the family." Ronnie's father shook Nate's hand. "Took you long enough."

"The best things in life are worth waiting for," he answered.

Yes, Ronnie thought, they were.

* * * * *

*Cowboy Grayson Cox is back in his hometown
with twin boys in tow. And he's stirring up all kinds
of feelings in local librarian Hadley Lanier!*

*Read on for a sneak preview of
THE COWBOY'S TEXAS TWINS,
part of Tanya Michaels's heartwarming
CUPID'S BOW, TEXAS series!*

As Hadley made her way toward the back of the store, a crash reverberated.

She heard a man's voice, followed by a high-pitched wail. Then a little boy yelled, "You made my brother cry!"

"Sam, I didn't— Tyler, don't… Boys, please!"

Momentarily abandoning her cart, Hadley peeked around the corner at the cereal aisle.

Boxes were everywhere. Among the cardboard wreckage, one boy sobbed facedown on the floor while another sat a few feet away, his eyes suspiciously dry. It took her a second to realize the boys were identical.

She cleared her throat. "Need a hand?"

The man whipped his head around. "Sorry about the disturbance, ma'am."

Flashing him a reassuring smile, she kneeled to retrieve a dented cereal box. "This hardly qualifies as a disturbance. You should see the library on story day when half the audience needs a nap."

He gave her a grin, and dimples appeared. *Oh, mercy!*

"What the heck happened here?"

Hadley glanced past Dimples to find a bewildered Violet Duncan.

The horizontal twin lifted his tearstained face. "It w-w-was a accident!"

"Grayson yelled at Sam!" the other twin accused.

Grayson…

Good Lord. Dimples was Grayson Cox? Hadley hadn't recognized her former classmate.

"I did not yell!" Grayson defended himself. "I told him to stop running, which he didn't, and then I pointed out the consequences of not listening."

Violet scooped up Sam and set him in the shopping cart. The action startled the boy out of his crying.

"If you and your brother will behave, you can come help me pick out something for dessert tonight." With a sigh, Violet turned to Grayson. "You want to finish restoring order here and meet us in the baking aisle?"

"Yes, ma'am." He ducked his gaze, looking as boyishly chagrined as young Sam.

When Hadley chuckled at his expression, all eyes turned to her.

Violet gave her a smile. "Hey, Hadley."

"Hadley?" Grayson echoed, turning back toward her. He blinked. "Hadley Lanier?"

She couldn't believe she hadn't recognized him sooner— or that she had yet to look away. *Quit staring.* Easier said than done. "I, uh… What was the question? Oh!" Her cheeks burned. "Yes. I'm Hadley."

Don't miss THE COWBOY'S TEXAS TWINS by Tanya Michaels, available February 2018 wherever Harlequin® Western Romance books and ebooks are sold.

www.Harlequin.com

HWREXP0118